The Ensign's Wife

MQ Pilling

iUniverse, Inc.
New York   Bloomington

iUniverse books may be ordered through booksellers or by contacting:

*iUniverse
1663 Liberty Drive
Bloomington, IN 47403
www.iuniverse.com
1-800-Authors (1-800-288-4677)*

*Because of the dynamic nature of the Internet, any Web addresses or
links contained in this book may have changed since publication and
may no longer be valid. The views expressed in this work are solely those
of the author and do not necessarily reflect the views of the publisher,
and the publisher hereby disclaims any responsibility for them.*

*ISBN: 978-1-4401-7716-3 (sc)
ISBN: 978-1-4401-7717-0 (ebook)*

Printed in the United States of America

iUniverse rev. date: 10/2/2009

Acknowledgement

Many thanks to R F Clough
Editor, Colleague, Scholar and Friend

Dedication

*To Betty Quealy, my mother and to
Stephanie Charles, my daughter.
Two strong, caring women whose love and
encouragement have shaped my life.*

Prologue

Venice 1661

"The Supreme Tribunal will see you now. The Duke is anxious to hear your news, dear cousin, and I am sure you are anxious to report all you know," Senator Brabantio himself took Lodovico's arm as the guard held the heavy wooden door opened.

"Anxious for the report on the tragedy in Cyprus? I wish that I had no news to report, much less be anxious to carry it to the Duke, Uncle." He stepped through the doorway.

Inside the grand chamber the three Inquisitors sat behind a long table. *Il rosso*, "the red one," wore scarlet robes; he had been chosen from the Dogal Councillors. The other two, in black, *i negri*, were appointed from the Council of Ten. Instituted in 1539, they were named a security body when the Hapsburgs threatened Venice. The three were responsible for maintaining vigilant internal surveillance, and carrying out espionage, and counterespionage for the Republic. Through a network of "confidants" they were privy to all the political and governmental intrigues. The Inquisitors were feared for their power and their information from informants, who could be bribed to give testimony against innocents: the victims of political vendettas. The events in Cyprus clearly fell under the interest of the Tribunal, as the murders were feared to be founded on acts of treason.

"Sit down before us, Signor Lodovico. Your uncle, Brabantio is overwrought at the news of his daughter's murder and wishes us to delve into the circumstances," *il rosso* spoke, as a scribe at a slanted desk off to the side recorded the proceedings on a scroll.

"Your Excellency, I will share what I know. It is still a confusion to me and I have been trying to organize my thoughts on my journey from Cyprus. I, too, mourn the loss of Desdemona deeply. My cousin did not deserve this outrage. I sensed that there was something seriously amiss as soon I entered the Governor's palace to deliver the letter from the Duke to General Othello." Lodovico bowed his head and shook it sadly.

"Go on," urged one of the black-robed inquisitors.

"The General seemed to be out of his humour. He was railing against his wife and seemed irrational. Desdemona greeted me and explained that her husband and his new lieutenant had fallen out. The entire company was filled with tension. Ensign Iago was the only man who seemed to have his wits about him. Then...then a most shocking thing..." he paused, seeming overcome with emotion.

"Please, Signore, try to be brief and to the point. Control yourself. We need the facts here in order to decide what is to be done." This time the scarlet-robed gentleman spoke sternly. His fists were clenched on top of the long polished table. "Continue!"

"He struck her. The innocent was thrown down." Lodovico's face reflected shock. He seemed stunned.

"Please, Signor, who struck whom? You must make sense." *il rosso* was losing his patience.

"The General was raving after he read the letter recalling him to Venice. Perhaps he had second thoughts about the appointment of Lieutenant Cassio to the governorship. He cried, 'Devil', and struck sweet Desdemona. He struck her!" Lodovico's shock turned to outrage as he shouted, "Othello sent her out heartlessly accusing her of false tears to win our sympathy. Old Brabantio would have seen him hung for this insult."

While the one black robe had remained silent, pondering all of this testimony, the other spoke again. "Very well. A dispute between a husband and wife. I am still unclear as to how this event led to the mutiny and treason, which resulted in the death of Brabantio's daughter and a citizen of Venice, one..." he referred to a document on the table before him, "Roderigo."

"Roderigo was a stranger to me, sir. He was a friend of the Ensign, I believe. At one point this Roderigo had pled a suit to Brabantio for Desdemona's hand and was rejected. That is all I know of this Roderigo." Lodovico was warming to his story, "Gratiano was witness to Othello's charges that his new wife, my cousin, had somehow betrayed him with the young lieutenant, but I am convinced that it was a ruse to create the chaos which would bring down the government of Cyprus. According to the one who survived, the Ensign's wife, Iago himself set the snare, invented the intrigue. She confronted him with his guilt and was stabbed for her efforts."

"And so you maintain that she was *not* an accomplice in the murder of Desdemona?" the silent one finally asked Lodovico the pivotal question.

"I am not sure that she is entirely innocent. She confessed at the scene of Desdemona's death that she stole a token that Othello had given his wife. She was following the orders of her husband. She openly accused Iago of manipulating Othello and indirectly causing the death of the young bride. The Moor was clearly enraged. Apparently Iago planted the handkerchief in the lieutenant's rooms to implicate him as the young girl's paramour. Outrageous. The girl was perfection. Purity itself." Again, Lodovico's voice caught in his throat. He was stricken at the waste, the tragedy, and the scandal.

"It is difficult to discern whether the Ensign's wife was part of the plot or merely a pawn in the deadly game," *il rosso* addressed an aid standing behind him. "She survived the knife wound, did she not?"

"Yes, Excellency, barely. She is in the Piombi awaiting her trial."

"In fact," he seemed satisfied, "Lodovico, the Duke has been entreated by his dear friend and colleague, Brabantio, to press this woman to the full extent of the law for treason and as an accomplice to the murder of his daughter. Unfortunately, the Ensign refused to speak even upon torture. So there are no witnesses to corroborate her own version of the intrigue. Gratiano himself applied the instruments of torture, but the sailor was adamant."

"Yes, Excellency, that is true. The Ensign, near death from the interrogation, was summarily hung as a traitor to the Republic." Lodovico had regained himself and spoke with authority. "Cassio, though wounded, has stayed to rule in Cyprus. He is well trained, but untested. We hope that things will go smoothly for him so that he may gain experience without further trial. As for the Ensign's wife, we will support your decision and that handed down by the Duke."

"Very well. You are excused." The Inquisitors had completed stage one of their inquiries.

Chapter One

*D*on Lorenzo had risen early to say mass in San Domenico, a vast structure with a single nave and a vaulted ceiling. It had been built in 1200 by the Dominican Order, but eventually the Jesuits had taken it over. Like most mornings, the marble floor seemed damp and any heat from the previous day had long ago risen to the pinnacle to be dissipated through the tile roof. As usual, he offered the early mass in the smaller side chapel as this service was meant to fulfil his daily office and provide the wives of Chioggia a community of prayer to bless the industry and safety of their men, the fishermen who had journeyed out to sea from the port at sunset. They would be arriving home soon with their catch, and the women would file out to the quay to greet them.

The women wore the *tonda* of white linen, which was a half skirt fastened round the waist and pulled up to cover the head and enclose the face. This costume made them resemble nuns, faces bound in the wimple of the convent. Lorenzo gave the final blessing and moved to the main altar to replace the paten, the cruets for water and oil, the chalice and to remove the host that he would carry with him today. The women remained kneeling, praying the rosary or taking time to savour the quiet before the workday began. Their solemn faces ranged from youngest wife of sixteen to the widows and grandmothers. Many left the side chancel and shuffled up the aisle to kneel before the main altar in homage to the most revered object in Chioggia: the miraculous crucifixion carved in wood.

There were two legends regarding its origin. The first story suggested that the cross was made by Christ's convert disciple Nicodemus, a witness to His death. The Crucifix then found its way to a town in the Marche region of central Italy. It is said that St. Peter Martyr asked to have it brought from there to Venice, and while in transit, a shipwreck caused it to wash up on Chioggia's shores.

Another legend claimed it to be one of four crucifixes made by St. Luke and that it was kept in Constantinople until 1453 when that city fell to the Turks. To prevent its destruction by the infidel, Christian soldiers threw it into the sea. "Divine will" then caused the precious cross to float to Chioggia.

The wooden carving was impressive; the sculpture of Christ was over three meters high, and the Cross measured more than five meters in height and nearly four meters wide. Although many in Chioggia viewed this realistic sculpture as the treasure of San Domenico. in Lorenzo's opinion the treasure of his church rested in the alcove of the second altar, the painting of St. Paul. A local painter, Carpaccio, had completed it and donated it to the church almost one hundred years before. The vibrancy of the colour and the haunting beauty of Paul's face touched Don Lorenzo. *"I am the Chosen Vessel,"* it seemed to echo in its majesty. Today the message seemed mocking.

"The Road to Damascus, indeed" Lorenzo thought. He dreaded the journey he must make today, only because it seemed to represent a personal failure as well as a tragic loss to the community.

The priest left the side entrance of San Domenico and passed over the canal of the same name on the Caletta Santacroce. He did not allow his eyes to try to penetrate the pre-dawn light or note the beauty of the quarter, lined with arcaded embankments and criss-crossed with smaller bridges which led to the Vena Canal, a main thoroughfare. Instead he hurried to the Ponte Sant'Andrea passed the fish market. Already men were moving large crates of fish, squid, eels, clams and mussels to the sloping racks for display.

Don Lorenzo followed the Corso, past the loggia of the granaries, a building drafted and erected by their own Matteo Caime. The priest crossed himself as he hurried by the shrine of Madonna and Child and passed the Municipal Palace. He had been there only last month to bless a meal hosted by the town magistrate. Now he recalled with irony the spectacle of the golden panel of *Justice between San Felice and San Fortunato*.

"Where was justice, felicity or fortune today?" he thought, as he turned into the Campo del Duomo. The bells began to toll from, the *campenile*, the tall bell tower; the priest quickened his step. It was late. Pasqualigo would be waiting for him.

The old sailor had agreed to transport him to San Giorgio Maggiore across from San Marco. Beneath his cloak the priest had the small vials of holy oil, the host in its compact golden pyx, his confessional stole and his breviary. The frayed purple ribbon marked the page for the ritual sacrament of Extreme Unction.

On the Peretolo Canal, Pasqualigo sat in his small fishing boat that would travel past the litorale di Pellestrina and turn into Malamocco. From there they would reach the Canale della Giudecca and land at the Isola San Giorgio Maggiore, where Don Lorenzo would stay with his old friend, Fra Paulo. On this small island the Benedictine monks had followed the sacred vows of poverty, chastity and obedience for centuries. The monastic life on this peaceful island, seemed suddenly compelling to Lorenzo. It would be a fitting place to contemplate and pray. There he could prepare himself for the visit to his beloved child of Christ, Emilia, kept in the Doges' Prison.

With a short greeting, Pasqualigo tapped out his pipe on the gunnels and set his oars. Don Lorenzo untied the hemp cable and carried it with him into the small boat. With his left foot he pushed firmly from the quay. His black robes dragged in the oily water at the bottom of the boat as he settled onto the plank. A freshening wind buffeted his wide-brimmed hat, as they approached the mouth of the Porto di Chioggia. Lorenzo pulled it firmly down to almost cover his eyes as they turned north.

It was just before dawn. The sky and sea met seamlessly as ribbons of rosy gold began to stream across the water from the East. Pasqualigo watched the island recede as his back moved into the familiar cadence of rowing. The old fisherman knew the purpose of the journey, but neither he, nor anyone on Chioggia, had asked for details or spoken above a whisper about the matter. Disgrace had fallen upon a respected family. That is all they need know. The memory of his hands pulled the right oar slightly harder as they glided past the the faccia of wooden masts roped together, which marked out the canals, the marine equivalent of sign posts on a road. These had an additional purpose of providing a resting place for the snakebird drying its wings in the dawn light, and a virtual housing complex for the barnacles, razor clams and mussels, some of the organisms who shared this watery world with men.

Less than one hundred years ago collecting salt had been the mainstay of the economy of Chioggia, named *Clodia* in antiquity. But when the course of the Brenta was altered, the harbour had filled with silt and this had changed the region into a fishing port. Soon Chioggia had become one of the major fishing communities of the Adriatic Sea. Situated between the open sea and the lagoon, Chioggia was surrounded by deep channels – the highways of the precious fish. Now the small fishing boats brought back the wealth from the sea.

Arriving in the busy harbour, each fishing smack transferred its cargo to a canoe-tender. The canoe swiftly thread the watery pathway, and shot alongside the *riviera della Pescheria*. The fish were then sorted upon marble slabs: the small fish in heaps, the large fish side by side. There each lot was auctioned to traders from the many inland markets. Each morning from the small shallow port, fish were sorted, sold in lots and shipped first to Venice and then on to other ports along the coast of Veneto.

The waters of the Adriatic had been good to the populous, but the water was changeable. The caprice of currents and tides had caused destruction, made the many wars possible, and generally held sway over the destiny of the Chioggiotti. These expert mariners were recognizable to the other island dwellers and the mainlanders by their heavy dark cloaks, stockings, and high wooden clogs. Large woollen hoods complimented their sun cured faces, lined and scarified like a map of the tributaries of the Po. Known as both valiant warriors and intrepid sailors, they were high-spirited and revelled in the many celebrations of the island. Their courage was mirrored in the proud and beautiful faces of their olive skinned mothers, daughters and wives.

Chioggia had maintained autonomy despite the strengthening power of the Venetian Republic. In the 8th century the government had been controlled by a Ducal Gastaldo. Later, a Grand Chancellor had superseded other magistratures. In 837 the Doge Pietro Tradonico defined the territory and outlined Chioggia's relationship with Venice; from then, through this *Pactum Clodiae*, Chioggia had shown its allegiance to the purposes of Venetian grasping. In critical moments even to the War of Chioggia in 1378, the Chioggetti fought the Genoese and suffered near destruction in order to save Venice, jewel of the Adriatic. Thus Chioggia, devastated and exhausted, fell from the prosperity and autonomy it had struggled so hard to maintain. Now the island followed the rising star of the greater city and the Venetian rule. Still admired for heroism and expertise in navigation, Chioggia was not merely a small moon pulled along by the steady planetary movements of Venice.

Lorenzo was lost in thought as he tried to piece together what had happened. As the Baseggio family priest, he had celebrated their successes, heard their confessions, baptized, confirmed and married their children – Stefano and Emilia. The *patrinus*, or *prin*, was regarded as confessor and spiritual advisor to the parishioner. Patrini and *compatres* or godparents, complemented one another. The godparents were responsible for guaranteeing the child's upbringing in the church. It was Lorenzo's role, as an ecclesiastic, to educate his parishioners in the ways of the church. He was also considered a close member of the household. Lorenzo had guided the Baseggio's in their faith and been present at every liturgical, familial and personal moment of their lives.

When Lorenzo had arrived in Chioggia after his ordination in Rome twenty eight years ago, he had been assigned as the young assistant to Father Bertoldus at San Domenico. Lorenzo had been especially taken with the Baseggio family and was delighted to be their spiritual guardian.

Vittorio Baseggio had carried on the family business of brokering the fish. His great grandfather, Eduardo Venerio, had gained his fortune from the lucrative salt panning on Chioggia. As that industry waned, he was able to transfer capital into the new commodity, fish, by buying rights to the fishing grounds surrounding several of the islands. "The sea giveth...," thought Lorenzo. Natalia Vernerio, granddaughter of Eduardo, had married Vittorio's father and with her dowry the family's empire grew. Vittorio' shrewd business acumen enabled him to secure still more fishing rights; and he had built a navy of fishing boats and hired an army of mariners only too willing to be his emissaries to the *Valli da pesca*. At low tide, when the waters would not yield fish, his boats would harvest the *velme*, marshland, for mussels that were so sweet they would hardly need the flavours infused into the rich soups by the housewives' herbs and the Baseggio catch was favoured as the freshest of the lagoon by the elite kitchens along the Grand Canal. Vittorio was sure that his harvest even graced the table of the Doge.

In his understated way, Vittorio was powerful; locally he was consulted and respected as an elder who could hold his own at the exchange of San Marco as well as at the smaller brokerages in the region. Like other businessmen and civic leaders, Vittorio Baseggio knew that the water levels were dropping and that care needed to be taken to protect the investment – the "farm". The delicate balance tipped with the extreme high tides which seemed to occur every five years. These were a grim reminder of the deadly waters that drowned almost a thousand Venetians two hundred years earlier as they left a fair from Mestre, the large town on the mainland opposite Venice.

Vittorio and other important men of the region also knew that the tide regularly rose above the stone foundations of the grand palaces and modest houses causing insidious, fundamental damage. Even the silky patina of Istrian stone was not impervious to the corrosive effects of salt. Following the *sirocco* wind, which carried red Saharan dust to the region in autumn, the tides would swell. With predictable regularity, the moon would pass over the meridian; and when the earth, moon and sun aligned, disaster would occur. Not the sudden disaster of the *terremoto*, earthquake, but the inexorable disaster of the slowly rising waters. The populous of Venice and its surrounding islands, whether rich or poor, would battle the *aqua alta*. Lorenzo smiled cynically as he thought, "Not the softest, richest leather, nor the rudest wooden clog would protect the feet from getting wet during the 'high water'." And always the push and pull. The give and take: sediment and erosion. "Nothing stays the same. All is changing."

Vittorio Baseggio had courted Faustina Sartore, the middle daughter of Bartolomeo Sartore, a wealthy cloth merchant on the northern island of Burano. Their wedding was cause for a colourful, week-long celebration of music, food and family. Lorenzo's mentor, the old Jesuit Michele, had officiated and loved to tell the elaborate story of Vittorio arriving on a decorated boat, the rich tapestries and woven silk carpets hanging from the windows of every pastel coloured house on the narrow waterways of Burano. He told of Faustina's nonna and mother crying tears of joy into the handiwork of their splendid lace kerchiefs and how he had eaten the rich dishes and drunk the fresh Veneto wines continuously for five days, only stopping long enough to accept the many bequests and generous donations for masses to be offered to bless the union.

By the time Vittorio and Faustina had settled into their home in Chioggia, life had quickened in Faustina. However, the old Michele had been laid to his eternal rest in the crypt of San Domenico, so it was he, Don Lorenzo, who had prayed with Vittorio the night his son was born. Stefano was brought to Vittorio by the midwife, who was smiling broadly and showing the red and wizened infant like a prize *maialino*, piglet! Faustina was well and resting after her long labour and Vittorio proclaimed that the whole of the mornings' catch be grilled, marinated, fried or poached and served with all the local side dishes on tables which stretched the length of the Campo del Duomo. Barrels of the local, coarse wine were rolled onto the steps of Santa Maria and the whole island toasted the newest Chioggiotti.

Stefano grew into a wonderful boy, unspoiled despite the attention showered on him by his mother and all the women of the quarter. In summer, he would be in Burano with his nonna and aunts and small cousins clamouring for sweets, flavoured ices, and rides in uncles' boats. The children roamed the edges of the narrow canals and were made dizzy gazing at perfect reflections of the crowded coloured houses in the still water. By the time Stefano was confirmed, he was known throughout the islands as a promising young man: bright, generous spirited, pleasing of face, well formed, and eager. He was his father's most precious treasure and Vittorio believed that the best way for his son to assume the responsibilities of the business was to be apprenticed to one of the expert fishers. Pasqualigo had been the one to teach Stefano about currents, patterns of the schools of fish, and the way to navigate even when stars were obscured by the low northern clouds. Pasqualigo had also initiated Stefano into the mysteries of that other world – women. Many housewives on the island hoped that their daughters would be chosen to marry Stefano.

Not only was he wealthy, but he was beautiful, gentle and fun loving. "The *raggazza* is like the fish. She teases you by swimming into your net, but will dart out if you try too hard or too soon to snare her. But if you are patient and even feign disinterest, she will chase you," he paused for effect, "until you catch her." The seasoned fisherman would smile around his pipe and crinkle his strange hazel eyes toward the sun, pondering all the fish and the women who had tempted his nets.

Near Stefano's second birthday, another son was born. But tiny Alessandro had only lived seven days. Lorenzo had knelt by Faustina's bedside praying as she nursed and willed the frail baby to live. He offered the funeral mass and the sadness of the tiny white coffin almost broke Vittorio's heart. Don Lorenzo sensed a hardening in Vittorio after this and the only time the tenderness returned was when Stefano was at hand to frolic and amuse and ask the childish questions that seem almost beyond philosophy to the parents who are confounded to answer. Faustina also suffered from Alessandro's death, but women are resilient. The Sorrows of the Virgin are the model for their forbearance; and, their faith in God instils trust. Soon the eight year old Stefano learned the responsibility of having a younger sister, and took on the role of the second man of the household. Emilia was born nine months almost to the day, from *Carnevale* in the year of 1625.

Don Lorenzo, himself, had grown up in a household of brothers and uncles in Padua. The ministry seemed a natural extension of the male world of his youth and his mother claimed that her prayers had been answered when Lorenzo acknowledged his vocation. St. Ignatius of Loyola had founded the Jesuit order. Lorenzo was drawn to the intellect and the anarchy of this order. The Jesuits would play the devil's advocate to the conservative clergy and even win the grudging respect, or perhaps fear, of the Popes.

At ten years of age, Lorenzo was keen enough to follow the talk of Pope Paul V's war with Venice. By the time he was 13 he had joined the seminary to embark on the arduous study of the priesthood. At twenty, Lorenzo was ordained in Rome, and his family travelled from Padua to view the solemn celebration. It was with surprise and relief that Lorenzo's appointment to Chioggia was received by his mother. His appointment kept him in the region of the Veneto; somehow she felt that he was safer for it. Although Lorenzo had struggled with pride and ambition and had imagined himself, God willing, in a post more prestigious or challenging than a small island on the lagoon of Venice, he settled easily into the rhythms of his parish and admired the strength and faith of his flock. His special association with Familia Baseggio was a particular joy and the birth of a daughter, Emilia, seemed an auspicious event.

She was like a tiny minnow of the lagoon – silvery, darting and lively. Don Lorenzo marvelled at her. She was baptized at the ancient font of carved marble in the alcove at the back of San Domenico when she was one month old. She was christened Emilia Madelena, her two grandmothers' names, as was the custom. When the priest handed the squirming bright-eyed infant to her godparents, she quieted; at that moment Lorenzo could have sworn that she looked into his eyes with a knowing gaze as if to say: I am yours to teach, and to care for and I will reward your efforts with my devotion to Our Lord.

Emilia, a restless baby, kept Faustina busy and fussing. Stefano handled his sister like she was a precious but hardy young lamb. He would jostle her, lift and bounce her, make her laugh until she could barely breathe and then moments later serenade her to sleep. Vittorio was less involved, but still doted on his children. When the merchants in Venice would ask him about his family, he would roll his eyes in mock distress and say, "*Tengo famiglia.*" I have a family; the traditional excuse for all married men. He beamed with pride and felt truly content.

Vittorio was often in Venice on business and away from Chioggia. Father Lorenzo would assume the role of protector in his absence. His special affection for Emilia was not lost on Faustina and she felt that it made up for some of the distance she sensed in Vittorio's relationship with his daughter. Lorenzo would watch Emilia mimicking her mother's movements around the house. Faustina encouraged Emilia to stand on a chair and roll out a small ball of pasta dough with her. The young girl was attentive to her religious lessons and seemed to relish that time of day when Lorenzo would read her stories from the New Testament or Lives of the Saints. However, he was careful to omit the most horrific descriptions of the martyrdoms, fearing it would frighten the child.

As she grew older, Emilia proved an eager pupil in other ways. Soon Emilia was preparing all the foods, the breads, tending the small kitchen garden, carefully pruning the herb plants and picking the fruit at just the right moment for its peak of sweetness. She followed the skill of her mother's hands as they used a needle and bobbin to fashion the strips of delicate lace that would be sold or used to trim the simple linen on a shelf or on a shawl. On Burano it was known that the art of lace making was a valued secret passed only from mother to daughter. Emilia learned quickly and nimbly; she mastered all the homely talents.

Yet, Lorenzo was reassured to note that Emilia had a mischievous and strong-headed side. He did not want to imagine her as submissive or dull. He knew, from the Stefano's confessions, that her doting brother had helped her don a dark cape, tuck her hair into a red wool hat, and pose as a fisher's apprentice. Stefano had taken her out in a *sandoli*, one of the small fishing boats that sailed along the Fossa Clodia, the lagoon which connected the island to the Lombardy region. They ventured to the Lusenzo, the customary harbour for fishing boats lying at anchor, and there they unwrapped coarse, dark unsalted bread spread thickly with the *bacala manteca*, the savory white mashed garlic, boiled cod and oil that was a typical lunch of the fishers.

The superstition of the mariners would have forbidden this intrigue. Several times men on the quay had asked the priest to bless a fishing boat that a woman had boarded in her haste to haggle for a catch. Women setting foot on the working boats was considered bad luck. Moreover, the local sumptuary laws were strict concerning dress. Each guild required members to wear a smock emblazoned with the particular emblem; each member of the community was bound to be straightforward in costume. For a young girl to dress as a boy was shocking and illegal.

But Emilia could cajole her brother and rationalize any scheme that would enable her to experience all aspects of his life. She adored him; at times she wished she had been his brother and had more freedom. Stories of the recent success of Clara in her suit to inherit Ca' Mosto above the distant uncles thrilled Emilia. The men sucked their teeth and shook their heads in simmering anger in telling the story of the wife of Giulio Dona, the bold woman who had challenged the traditions of progeny and inheritance. They were indignant on behalf of the last male in the cadet branch of Marco da Mosto's descendants when the courts ruled in favor of the last offspring in the senior line of Marco: a daughter, Clara. The power and attention that the tenacious woman had gained fascinated Emilia.

However, as she grew older, Emilia only aspired to be like other women of Chioggia: to be given to a good husband, make him proud of her abilities to run a house, provide him with the best dishes and to give him healthy sons.

Faustina tried to explain the real power that women have. "The man is the head, Emilia," she said, "but the woman is the *neck*!" The other women in the garden listening to this statement threw back their heads and laughed at the wisdom of this adage.

Don Lorenzo had confirmed Emilia when she was of age, knowing that soon after he would help her father broker her marriage to a man of consequence. A good man. A man of great intelligence, loyalty and honour.

"The man, in fact, who had a month earlier, been arrested, remained silent under torture, and been put to death for murder and treason," thought Lorenzo, ruefully.

Chapter Two

Emilia was dreaming. Her soft moans were swallowed by the heavy tapestries hanging over the stone walls. Her bed was a wooden affair strung with ropes, and the mattress was stuffed with wool and straw. Bits of the straw would work through the homespun linen cover and the wool had formed knots or lumps in the sacking. Still, she slept deeply and feverishly. Her wound ached and seeped, but had become less bothersome. She had been back in Venice for almost a month, recovering and answering for her crimes. Her lawyer was a kindly old man, who alternately reassured her and prepared her for the worst. He brought a doctor to redress her wound and he had obtained special permission for a woman to minister to her. The old Venetian midwife knew how to mix herbs and make the poultice that would be applied to her wound. It had only been in the last weeks that Emilia became lucid and had begun to comprehend what was happening to her.

She vaguely recalled the journey from Cyprus on a boat, and being carried on a litter up a labyrinthine staircase through the halls to this chamber. Then there was a dulled memory of pain – a searing pain. She thought she might have cried out. She found it painful even now to straighten her body completely on the cot, or to try to rise upright. Her mouth felt dry and her lips were cracked and sore. At night her eyes would seal shut with a gummy weeping; but, having them shut seemed easier than trying to focus in the dim light. She was floating in her dream. Floating in a pool - someone was holding her waist to keep her afloat. She could not discern the face. She only knew that she felt safe and that the hands were gentle.

She woke with a start calling, "Mamma. Mamma." Real tears released her lashes from the sticky pus and she opened her eyes on the familiar ceiling of her cell. She had learned the textures of the stone. Counted the crevices and seams. Noted the lightly coloured moss or lichen that had grown there, sustained by the damp breath of prisoners like herself, or perhaps generated by the tiny creatures that travel on the mist from the waterways. A narrow window with leaded panes permitted scant light to fall across the floor, work its way up the western wall and pass out of the room – all within what she tried to calculate to be four hours. Small puffs of wind would pass through the opening underneath the door, but the room was close and smelled of her bandages and her sweat.

She wanted to sleep. She only felt safe when she slept and could forget. Or was she trying to remember? But to remember something better than the nightmare. She let herself drift back to sleep and soon a dream unravelled to envelop her.

She was twelve and Stefano brought the bundle to her mother's room. It contained the costume provided by the richest family of the parish. Mama carefully unwrapped the dress and slips, the veil, stockings, shoes, shawl. The fabric seemed alive like the fishes in the nets: glistening and changing from silver to gold to burnished blue. The shawl was a soft violet with intricate embroidery of metallic threads in delicate patterns of flowers and leaves and tiny coloured birds. The edges were tasselled threads of violet and silver. She had never seen anything so beautiful. Her mother had pulled and brushed and braided her hair until she thought she would cry with the pain of both the brushing and of the need to be so still. It was not in her nature to be still for very long, but today was important. It was an honour; and she had been chosen amongst all the girls in her parish; she was to represent the island as the "Mary." Emilia was nervous and proud; and secretly believed that she was the only choice they could have made. She was the best girl on the island! She had learned her catechism more quickly and thoroughly than any of the others. She had been able to work side by side with her mother to prepare the feasts, decorate the boats, greet any visitors to their house.

She had brought only honour to the family. She knew that Don Lorenzo had been part of the decision and that made her feel a bit more humble. The most frequent sin that brought her to confession was pride. Now she could add vanity to the list. Pride, disobedience, and now vanity. She gazed at her reflection in the glass above the credenza and thought she was looking at a stranger through a window. And today would be her first visit to the mysterious Venice. The Venice that pulled her father away from them so frequently. The Venice of the most extravagant and outrageous carnival celebration. The Venice of the

Grand Canal and palaces and the Duke! Don Lorenzo had told her of the Basilica San Marco and the beauty of its decoration. "Even the floor is magnificent," he had said.

The velvet shoes embroidered with golden thread, *Could it be real gold?*, pinched her heels slightly, but she would not allow herself to notice. Her mother placed the special rose gold and ruby earrings in her ears. These were the earrings her mother had worn as a bride and had belonged to her grandmother's grandmother! She had only been allowed to hold them once. Now she was wearing them. They twinkled behind the silky strands that trailed from her crown of braids. She wished all her cousins in Burano could see her today. And especially Dario.

"Come. It is time," her father called from the salon. Her mother followed her down the staircase, holding her veil carefully away from the floor. Don Lorenzo was standing next to her father. Don Lorenzo crossed himself and her father caressed her head with such tenderness that she felt tears come into her eyes. "How beautiful you look!" exclaimed Stefano who had just rushed through the door. He took her hands in his and gently twirled her around.

"My beautiful little sparrow, now you are like the colourful Kingfisher – all blue and sparkling and shining!" Stefano escorted her and the rest of the family followed like a duchess's entourage. He gently lifted her into the boat which would take them to Venice. There she and the other twelve most beautiful young girls of Venice would ride in gondolas to San Pietro and be blessed by the bishop. Then they would proceed to San Marco for Mass to commemorate the Feast of the Purification of the Virgin. Finally in lavishly decorated barges, they would follow the Doge's barge up the Grand Canal, past all the richest palaces that would be decorated with banners, tapestries and flags, as far as the Rialto Bridge. There, by Santa Maria Formosa, a grand feast would be served to celebrate the rescue of the Venetian brides from the pirates seven hundred years before.

Don Lorenzo and all the other parish priests would present the Doge with the traditional gifts of gilded straw hats, flasks of malmsey wine and baskets of oranges. Emilia was seated on a long bench opposite the other richly costumed girls. She was being presented with a cup of the sweet wine. She tried to lift her head toward the cup but something was pressing on her.

"Signora, try to drink. Please, madame. It will make you stronger." Her eyes focused and the pale face of the nurse swam before her. The warm broth trickled into her mouth. She tried to swallow. "Yes, yes, that is the way. Take a bit more," the woman cooed softly and gently tipped more of the warm liquid into Emilia's mouth. It was sweet and salty at the same time and she could faintly smell the herb, thyme.

"The lawyer will come soon. He will explain the procedures of your meeting with the Inquisitors. Dottore Santacroce is a good man. He will represent you well." She was straightening Emilia's bed clothes and smoothing her hair. "You need to try to sit up, Signora. It is not good to lie flat for so long. It is not good for the lungs." She hoisted Emilia up on the pillows and raised her shoulders, propping them. The movement stretched the healing wound and Emilia thought she might faint from the pain.

"No. No. Please. I cannot." The change of position made her heart race and her head felt light. She thought she might be sick. Her skin felt clammy and beads of perspiration sprang out on her forehead.

"Wait, Signora. I will fix it." The nurse had a shallow pan of water at the ready and began to put cool compresses against Emilia's head and cheeks. The nausea passed and Emilia merely felt sore and exhausted. The woman had propped open the cell door and a fresh breeze wafted into the room causing the dampness on Emilia's face to evaporate quickly and lower her temperature. A guard stood a few meters off, outside the door. He knew this prisoner was not a threat in terms of escape. Besides, this was the *Piombi* section of the prisons. In this section the cells were meant for prisoners awaiting sentencing and for those who were incarcerated for a short period of time. The *Pozzi*, or "wells" area below was for hardened criminals. The Venetian rule had done away with torture and cruelty as part of punishment. The idea was to cause a more psychological suffering which would encourage remorse and even rehabilitation. *Piombi* was so named for the lead shield of the building's roofing and these cells were just below that roof.

Emilia was floating again. This time she was lying back in a small gondola. The sky above was the dark cerulean blue of the Adriatic islands. Her eyes travelled down and she recognized the pastel coloured houses of her mother's island, Burano. It was her last summer there as she was of an age now that she would stay close to home for her betrothal. Her eyes filled with tears at the thought and she stared at the slim, solemn figure of her beloved Dario. He was at the oar of the gondola and they had just had a quiet lunch in his mother's kitchen. Signora Soranzo adored Emilia and would have been very pleased to welcome her into her family as Dario's wife, but she was too realistic to hope for such a thing. Emilia's family was important and she would require an important match – a commercially and politically wise union. She had heard from Faustina's sister that Signor Baseggio had already interviewed several suitors. When the youngsters left the small piazza in front of the house to take the bark and float in the narrow waterways of Burano, she turned back to her kitchen and picked up her *tombola*, the cushion she used in her lace making, sighing at what she knew would cause her son pain.

Emilia sat up in the gondola and stared hard at Dario's face. His hat shaded his eyes and she could not see them, but she felt him returning her gaze. They had passed from the most populated part of the island and were travelling toward the *Fondamente del Squeri* on the outside edge of the northwest top of the island. Here Dario would tie the small flat bottomed boat to one of the striped poles that projected out of the water for that purpose. Then he would clamber to the front of the boat and lower himself on the cushions beside Emilia.

They had taken to this ritual in the last days of August last summer. Emilia had known Dario and his family since the first summers when her mother would return to the island and stay with her sisters. It was a small and lively place for the children to get to know their cousins and have a certain independence. On this quiet island the commerce was in the delicate lace and textiles; there was no bustling harbour with the myriad of local and foreign fisherman unloading and selling their wares as there was in Chioggia. The pace was slower here.

Dario had been a close school friend of Emilia's cousin, Andrea. Soon Dario and Emilia were inseparable. If anyone wanted to find one of the pair, they would certainly, then, find the other. At first Andrea seemed a little annoyed that his best friend had forsaken him for a girl; but he soon found another group of boys to call best friends. Dario and Emilia were like brother and sister: *risi e bisi*, "rice and peas", was what her mother called them. And, indeed, they were always together. Emilia looked forward all the year to her summer in Burano and freedom from the customary restraints placed on girls. She relished her time spent in tomboyish pursuits with Dario.

However, after her confirmation, Emilia sensed an awkwardness in their friendship. Dario was two years older and he was changing. Now their play had a different tenor. There was less horseplay and more conversation. It was improper now for Emilia to step out of her skirt, peel off her blouse and dive into the water off the pier at the small lido. Now she would lift her skirt and gently walk the edge of the pebbly sand, instead. One day last summer Dario announced that he had permission to take the boat on his own. And so while the rest of the island was resting, after the midday meal, they drifted and took turns rowing, exploring every tiny rivulet that would accept the narrow boat. Then one day Dario tied the boat to the pole at quay and lay down beside her. She felt her insides tighten. There was an aching that she could not identify when he placed his hand on her stomach, very casually, very lightly. She turned to look into his pale hazel eyes. They were like Stefano's eyes, she thought. It was the first time she had noticed this.

She was so intent on this revelation, that Dario took her by surprise when he leaned toward her face and softly pressed his lips to her mouth. He quickly pulled away to see how she had received this boldness. Emilia began to smile and then to laugh a little. If this was a new game for them, then so be it. She kissed him back. Dario turned his whole body to hers and pressed against her. She felt herself become as fluid as the seagrass. She was floating. She could not breathe. The feeling was so delicious, so beautiful and tender that it never entered her mind that it could lead to sin.

And so it happened that the unspoken goal of every afternoon was to end up here. End up in each other's arms exploring the sensations of kissing, touching and holding. Emilia knew that she was in love with Dario. Dario had always known he was in love with Emilia. Neither one considered the reality of society's plans for them. The world was encompassed within the rude wooden gunnels of this small flat-bottomed boat floating at the end of a cord. Nothing beyond that mattered.

"Signora. Signora! Please open your eyes. You must pay attention." Santacroce needed to consult with his client directly and it had to be today. She and she alone could fill in the details of the events that had occurred in Cyprus. He had been visited on several occasions by her brother Stefano, who controlled the family business, but there had been nothing to report and no answers to be found. Although old Baseggio maintained his position as a figure-head of the family, he was of little use now. He was devastated by the betrayal of the man who had promised to love and care for Emilia – her husband to whom she had been so devoted, so giving. In return this husband had tried to kill her outright.

"But the details," muttered the lawyer, "the details! Signora, please listen to me!" He threw up his hands and looked beseechingly to the nurse. The doctors had done all they could to keep her alive and would only be called in later – to confirm her death.

"I will try to rouse her. I know that she is anxious to tell you. One moment." Again, the nurse swabbed Emilia's face and jostled her slightly, thinking it would bring her around, even if it was pain that did the trick.

Was it her father? Could he have forgiven her crimes and come to her side. Emilia strained her eyes and moved to rise off the cot. "Poppi! Poppi!" "So! Finally we have you with us, my dear." But that was not her father's accent. "I must ask you to recite all that you can recall of the intrigue. Your husband is gone and he can no longer harm you. You are safe, my child. Tell me what role you were forced to play in this shocking affair." The lawyer drew a chair close to the cot.

"Desdemona. My beautiful Desdemona. She is gone." Emilia began to sob and all the tears that had been held back by her body's natural healing response, came out in a rush. She could not stop them.

"Good. That is good. This shows that you have remorse. That you did not plan to harm her. To save you we must convince the court that you were merely an innocent pawn in his diabolical plan." The lawyer nodded and rested his hand on her arm.

At this, Emilia began to understand that Iago was dead, too. He had been led away under guard after her outcry against him. She had loved him. Still loved him. She understood him and was his wife. Emilia did not believe he had a tendency for cruelty, but he had been wronged; he had become something that was unnatural. She knew he was not a traitor. He was loyal to Venice and had given his whole life to protecting the state. Her tears mingled with a deep sadness for him, for his wrongs and for wrongs committed against him.

She felt herself drifting back in her mind to that other place – that other loss.

After that last magic summer with Dario, Emilia's father had her brought back to Chioggia. Emilia was in mourning for the end of her summers with Dario. Faustina talked to her about duty, obedience, responsibility and honour. Her mother had some inkling of the closeness that had developed between her daughter and the Soranzo boy, but she knew, too, that her daughter was a good girl. The intensity of their closeness had not spoiled her daughter. "In fact, it was important for Emilia to understand the power a woman has over a man in passion," she thought. "Emilia is taking those first lessons in how to please her husband."

For her part, Emilia knew she was expected to follow the path that had been set for her even from her birth. She wanted that. But she could not accept the loss of Dario as part of the plan. Love-marriage was not considered; if one developed love after the wedding and if that love sustained the couple over the many years, that was fortunate. Stefano had married well and he and Maria Giustiana were very happy. Giustiana had become like a sister to her. But Emilia wondered if Stefano could love his wife in the way that Emilia loved Dario. Stefano sensed Emilia's sorrow and came to her; as he had done all of her life, he tried to explain what was expected.

"You will always have Dario. You are his and he is yours. But your husband is something else. He holds sway over you and you must bend to him. I know that you will be a loyal wife for any worthy man. Let yourself accept this and you will find happiness and peace. Think of your children and your chance to be like our mamma. She did not know our father at all until their wedding day and look at how they respect and support each other. Consider the beautiful children they have made." He laughed at his little joke and this made her smile, too.

She knew in her heart that Stefano was right, but something was dying inside of her. She felt desperate when she realized that she was slowly losing the ability to conjure Dario's sweet face. To imagine his eyes, his kisses and caresses. "No," she thought, "Never! I will *never* forget him." She vowed that when she lay with her husband on their marriage night, in her heart, it would be Dario who would receive her.

Emilia remembered the first time she had seen Francesco Gradenigo, It was at the war of the sticks on the Campo San Barnaba. At the time, of course, she had no idea that he was to become her husband.

The family had travelled to Venice for the grand marriage of Stefano to Maria Giustiana. The ceremony was to take place in the Santa Maria dei Miracoli. Don Lorenzo had been invited by the Patrinus of the Famiglia Foscari to celebrate the wedding mass. Giustiana's family was one of the most important in Venice and the marriage should have occurred in San Marco, but Giustiana was her father's jewel and she had persuaded him to agree to a more humble setting: this unusual church dedicated to the Immaculate Conception and nestled on a small canal. The Madonna was a favourite icon of the young girl and she loved the tranquillity of this quarter of Venice.

The Campo di Santi Giovanni e Paolo was where Emilia and her family disembarked. They waited by the well-head in the center of the campo, the well which was famous for its clear sweet water. Ferries and smaller gondolas docked at the landing continuously and soon the others in the groom's family had arrived from the island of Burano. Emilia's aunts, uncles and all of the cousins were coming to witness the great union. The campo was filled with people, all the many guests there to celebrate Stefano's marriage. At the sound of the herald, the grand procession filed passed the majestic equestrian statue in the Calle Larga Gallina toward the smaller square of Santa Maria Nova. They paraded into Santa Maria dei Miraboli. The painting above the altar was the magnificent, miracle-working image of the Madonna.

Emilia thought the church resembled a dowry chest from Constantinople she had seen once at the dock in Chioggia. The inside of the domed lid had been painted with icons and the interior of the chest depicted finely detailed scenes. The church was the same and she had to restrain from tipping her head back and from side to side to take in the paintings of the holy men across the coffered ceiling.

Stefano looked solemn at the front of the church and the image of the Virgin seemed to be considering the pageant from above the altar. Giustiana's father led her through the nave to the transept where Stefano stepped forward to accept her hand from her father. They climbed the stairs to the tribune and stood facing the altar. Giustiana looked stiff and nervous, but beautiful in her Indian damask gown of deep red, edged with a border of gold meander. Her headdress was of the same rich fabric, but tiny pearls created a floral pattern around the crown and the meander in gold on the band that secured it to her head. Gold mesh encased her thick dark hair in a snood that rested on the back of her neck. The pointed sleeves of her gown almost covered her hands, but fluting at the wrist softened the effect.

Giustiana had the fine features and the almond shaped eyes of the Venetians. The creamy skin of her throat created a striking contrast to the colour of the dress. Stefano's olive skin looked swarthy against her alabaster fingers as he took her hand in his. The mass proceeded, and they knelt side by side to receive communion and stood to recite the vows of Holy Matrimony. The solemnity of the service quickly evolved into the raucous and almost hedonistic display of wealth in food and wine at the feast. All of the traditional dishes were prepared for the several hundred guests. There were many delicacies from the seas, meats and fowl from the Veneto, the sweets and savory nutmeats that were typical of celebration.

The Ca' Foscari, the family's palace on the Grand Canal, easily provided space for the extended Baseggio family and they stayed in Venice for a week, allowing Emilia to view and embrace this city of wonders. Her cousin Andrea was to chaperone her wanderings, as he was more familiar with the labyrinthine streets and small squares of the six districts or *sestiere* that comprised the six administrative divisions of Venice. Each of these *insulae* or small territories surrounded by a river or canal was connected to another by the bridges over the many canals and each district had its particular flavour or function. It could be a magnificent church on a quiet square, or an elegant palace on a canal, or a district could be significant as a market area.

So Andrea led her in their exploration of the mysterious city. Andrea showed Emilia the Canneregio district, named for its early function as a marsh where cane was grown. Now it was the sight of the Gothic masterpiece of Ca'd'Oro, the golden palace. This district was also the location of the Jewish ghetto. Andrea and Emilia wandered the alleys, where the Jews were sequestered behind gates and a drawbridge each sundown; the curfew was lifted at sunrise with the tolling of the *marangano*, the bell named for the guild of carpenters.

Following the Strada Nuova they arrived at Rialto Bridge and joined the masses of Venetians who thronged the canal where gondolas stacked with fruits and vegetable plied their wares. Beyond that busy thoroughfare, they found themselves in the quieter district of Madonna dell'Orto – Our Lady of the Vegetables – and stopped briefly in the church of that name to see the paintings by the famous artist Tintoretto. Taking a narrow alley they ended up in a small square which opened up to a view across the waters to the Island of San Michele, the cemetery island of the lagoons.

They retraced their steps and passed by the Campo Santa Maria Formosa before they ended up where the visitor inevitably ends up in Venice – the grand square of San Marco.

"After this we must head back to Ca'Foscari," Andrea said. "But I am hoping to meet a friend from Burano near San Marco." Almost as soon as the small street opened into the square a young man approached Andrea and greeted him.

"Ciao! Are you ready for tomorrow?" The boy acknowledged Emilia with a small bow. "You are Emilia, Andrea's cousin. I know of you from my friend Dario. I am Raffael. Welcome to Venice." He turned back to Andrea and spoke excitedly, "The spectacle lasts most of the day and I know you will enjoy it. Shall we try to meet?"

"If the battle is as popular as you say, we may not find each other. But we can meet here later after the event," Andrea's face was animated. They agreed on their plan. Raffael smiled at Emilia, excused himself and walked briskly toward the seafront.

Once Andrea and Emilia were on their own again, she asked Andrea what it was all about. He told her he would explain later. Now he needed to get her back to Ca' Foscari for lunch and repose. She begged him to allow her to take a moment to enter the Basilica. So they ended their day's tour by lighting a candle and kneeling in the cool emptiness of the cavernous Basilica San Marco. Emilia had not been inside church since she had been a "Mary" three years earlier. Then she had hardly been able to take in the beauty of it, there had been such a press of people and she had been so conscious of her own role in the pageant. Again, her vanity. She made a special prayer to ask forgiveness for her sins through the intercession of the patron saint of this magnificent city. She also prayed for Stefano and Giustiana - a happy marriage and many children for them.

Chapter Three

*D*uring the late afternoon promenade Emilia made sure she was walking with Andrea. They dropped back from the others and she pressed him to tell her about the spectacle that he and Raffael had discussed that morning. He began to tell her the history of this event.

"Long ago, when Henry, the King of France, visited Venice, the local governor and all the nobles made a procession with the King and his entourage. They stayed at Ca' Foscari, as a matter of fact." Emilia had heard that Giustina's ancestors had included a Doge, but to be staying in the same palace where the King of France had stayed thrilled her.

Andrea continued. "On the 19th of July the King was feted. And on the 26th, which falls tomorrow, the

Venetians staged a *guerra de' canne*, or war of the sticks. It was meant to impress and perhaps even frighten the French group a bit. It showed the ferocity and skill of even the artisans and common classes of the city. And more than that the little battle was fought on a bridge." Andrea looked hard at Emilia. "I suppose it is not savoury for a young girl to witness the battle, but I will take you to it, if you promise not to faint or tell your mother. Well?"

"Oh, yes, yes. Please do take me, Andrea. Please. I feel like so much of my life is over because of all the rules about what a young lady may see, or do and may not." Her vehemence surprised Andrea, who had always thought of his little cousin as a reserved and obedient girl.

"All right. I will come for you in the morning and we will go along as if we are merely continuing our exploration of Venice. Agreed?" She nodded solemnly. She yearned to ask Andrea for any news about Dario, but sensed it was not the right moment, so she left him and walked more quickly to join the group as they ended their walk and settled for an *aperitivo* before the late dinner. They stopped at a small café that Signor Foscari knew. The men entered the dark rooms, while the women sat at round marble tables under a portico beside the water. She was served a dish of *cicheto*, bites of salt-cod, but yearned instead for a glass of flavoured ice. The women were discussing the fashions at the wedding. The men usually had a fried sardines in a sweet and sour sauce, and thin slices of the Venetian dried ham. They drank glasses of pinkish fizzy wine and talked of business and politics.

That night, in the high ceiling room that she shared with her girl cousins, Emilia could hardly sleep thinking of the King, the battle she would see the next day, and Stefano and his new life. He would be living in Venice now, and Emilia wondered if she would see much of him. She knew he would try to help her and to advise her, as he had always done, but she knew the business would keep him away, as it had taken her Poppi away from Chioggia. She missed Stefano already and felt tears roll down the sides of her eyes to the pillow. Why did everything have to keep changing? Was she destined to lose everyone she loved?

Early the next morning Andrea pulled Emilia through the crowds clogging the narrow streets of the Dorsoduro district which linked the Ca' Foscari with the Campo Santa Margherita and the Rio di San Barnaba. Soon they approached *Ponte di Pugni*, or Bridge of Punches. The area was swarming with people. Even the impoverished religious women who sheltered in the portico of San Nicolo' dei Mendicoli, were pushed aside to accommodate the crowds surging toward the Campo San Barnaba hoping to find a good vantage point from which to watch the battle, or *spettacolo vile.*

The battle was named *guerra de' canne* after the long rattan sticks used as weapons. These were about a meter in length, tapered and sharpened at the business end. The points had been repeatedly immersed in boiling oil to temper them into strong lances. The combatants ranged from butchers and fishermen to shipbuilders and sailors of the city. Various battles were to take place over the day, each one ending in bloodshed, opponents ending up over the bridge in the canals, or being joined by various overzealous and wine soaked spectators. Some clans used the occasion of the *guerra de' canne* to settle the scores on long running vendettas. Whole groups of men and boys from one family would flood over the bridge to face and battle another mob. These free for alls often ended in serious injury, which would then be fuel for the continuation of the vendettas to the next year. But overall, the war of sticks was a way for the working classes to offer entertainment and a show of loyalty to the aristocracy of Venice. It was a way of tacitly saying: We are ferocious and we are willing to fight for the honour of our city. Some combatants wore light helmets and carried a light shield. Some even wore a type of chain mail, but this was risky as it could sink you if you were knocked off the bridge into the waters.

Andrea pushed Emilia ahead of him and, because she was small, people were willing to allow them to edge to the front. Andrea held her firmly in front of himself to prevent her from being pushed into the canal as they prepared to watch the spectacle. Soon a drum rumbled and a pair of gladiators mounted the bridge from opposite ends. The first battle was fierce and ended with one opponent having a tooth knocked out and the other suffering a glancing blow to the head which caused a good deal of blood to spill into his eyes before he was hefted over the rail into the canal. A great shout rose from one side of the crowd and catcalls and whistles emitted from the group just behind Andrea and Emilia.

The next battle went similarly. Both combatants were well armed with shields, sticks and helmets. The fighting seemed to go on and on. The July heat caused a noxious smell to rise from the edges of the canal. Emilia thought it would be awful to be thrown into this oily water. Sludge from all the streets and latrines flowed freely into the canals, as well as old fish water and bits of vegetables from the markets being swept into the waters. She looked down at the water just below her and saw the carcass of a common resident in Venice: *il pantegana*, a large rat. She felt bile rise to her throat and swayed toward the edge of the water. Just as she was about to ask Andrea to lead her away, a tremendous shout went up from the crowd to their right. Emilia recognized their costumes as that of the sailors in the Venetian navy. On the bridge stepped two men who looked very evenly matched. Both had forgone the helmet and wore only a white kerchief to hold their hair out of their eyes. Their simple white stockings and the low, soft boots were common to the sailors. White shirts flowed over short black pantaloons and these were topped by deep red vests bearing the crest of the service.

The battle started and the first crack of the cane tore through the sleeve of the darker of the two. He promptly, and in mid-swipe of returning the cut, tore off his shirt and vest in one movement. He was tanned and his muscles strained and bunched as he lunged at his opponent. The other man was a bit thinner and taller with a reddish mop of straight hair. Finally, he also released his arms from the constriction of his white blouse. Instead of throwing it aside, he wrapped it around his other arm and waved it in the face of his opponent in an attempt to draw his attention away from the battle. His strategy did not work and a loud crack of the cane opened a wound on the thinner man's shoulder. Blood streamed across his chest and mixed with the sweat that had already caused his skin to sheen like the surface of a polished wooden table. His face did not betray any pain or concern and he lunged and fought until the stronger looking man was pressed against the rails of the bridge.

Suddenly the dark opponent jumped backward and mounted the stone rail. The crowd let out a roar and more cheers to urge them on. The thinner man's cane flashed and sliced into the other man's cheek, opening a gash that began dangerously near his eye and extended almost to his jaw. This incensed the darker sailor and he fought even harder. The thinner man had not counted on the ferocity that would ensue after this insult and was soon pinned to the stones on the bridge with his hand reaching up in supplication as his cane was thrown clear.

The crowd cheered and the dark, strong man leapt again on the stone rail in triumph. He turned, raised his arms and performed a mocking deep bow toward his supporters. As he raised his head, he looked straight into Emilia's eyes and his triumphant smile seemed to widen, showing all of his even white teeth. Emilia was clapping and smiling back. It was the first battle that had clearly been won and she had been caught up in the excitement. He turned to his friends to her right and they broke into cheers and began singing a victorious battle song. He pulled off his bandana and a cascade of black, ringlets fell over his forehead. He swept his hand over his brow, not paying any attention to the gaping, streaming wound on his cheek and sprang from the edge of the bridge into the crowd, who deftly caught him and carried him away on their shoulders, singing and chanting: "Iago! Iago! Bravo! Bravo, Iago!"

Andrea pulled Emilia gently back from the edge of the crowd and suggested they go for a cool flavoured ice in the next piazza. He was unsure if bringing Emilia here would backfire on him or if she would be able to suppress the flush in her cheek and her excitement at the *spectacolo vile.*

"Signora, don't weep. I promise we will do all in our power to help you in your appeal to the Inquisitors. What role did you play in the treason? How did you help your husband in his intrigue? Signor Brabantio is determined that someone pay the price for the death of his daughter and you are here. The others met their end far away, out of his power. The Senator's vendetta has a hunger beyond reason, but the courts are bound by logic and justice."

Emilia knew that the lawyer was sincere in his intention to help her, but she herself was unclear of exactly what had been her role. Had she been the hinge upon which the disaster had swung, or had she only been a dupe? Her torn loyalties had prompted her to denounce her husband and bring a sort of truth into the open. Would anyone have known the truth if she had remained silent? After all, despite being an important General, Othello was an alien. The marriage of the Moor and Desdemona was considered by many as an abomination. It was not entirely unexpected that things would end badly. Desdemona was a head-strong and very young girl who had defied her father by eloping in the night. But Emilia knew that Desdemona loved Othello with all her heart. And from what Desdemona had told Emilia about Othello, she had thought the Moor was capable of returning the young girl's love. Something had changed him. Something had unleashed a passion capable of murder. How can one destroy the object of one's love? How could her own husband turn on her? The vitriolic power of that aggression was almost comprehensible when she thought back. But no, that was not the memory she wanted now.

"I will try to tell you," her voice was hoarse and faint from disuse. "I must sleep. I will tell you, but after…" Her head fell to the side.

"We have lost her again," said Santacroce. "What am I to tell her brother?" He threw up his hands and stood up abruptly. "It is no use."

Chapter Four

$\mathcal{P}$asqualigo took in the triangle of sailcloth that he had raised in the bow of the boat to aid in the journey. They had travelled the Litorale di Pellestrina and were turning into the Porto de Malamocco. Further inland from that port was the Laguna Morta. The lagoons were labelled *morta*, dead, or *viva*, living, to denote which lagoons were still and surrounded by silted marshlands and which lagoons were refreshed and renewed by tidal waters. On the Laguna Morta, basins, where salt water and rainwater mingled, created a brackish environment that was a perfect nursery for various mussels, prawns and crabs. The lagoons were criss-crossed with tiny canals that shifted and wandered through the small strips of land that appeared and then sank. These marshes were rich with vegetation: the Chioggian red leafed radicchio, glasswort and sea rocket.

It was ironic that these lagoons are labelled dead, thought Pasqualigo, as he looked up and recognized the long trailing legs of the grey heron flying overhead toward the west. The colourful water birds who nested in the reeds, the elegant strutting birds whose delicate, red legs picked through the brush as the long, curved beak sieved small crustaceans from the shallows, and the acrobatic kingfishers swooping and diving, were all familiar to the old fisherman. They had been his companions, markers for good fishing, and watchmen to signal winds or weather. The waters of Laguna Morta were, in fact, teeming with life above and below the surface.

The boat tacked hard as the sail came down and Pasqualigo scrambled to retrieve the oars from Lorenzo who had held them steady. They began to travel up the inland canal to the Canale della Giudecca and on to the Isola di S. Giorgio Maggiore, where Lorenzo's Benedictine would give them lunch. After a rest, Pasqualigo would turn back south to Chioggia. He would have discharged his duty to the priest and to the Famiglia Baseggio. He crossed himself.

Lorenzo began to feel the excitement he always felt when he approached Venice. In spite of himself and his mission, Venice made his pulse quicken. Jesuits were never assigned to San Marco, *that* he had known since his time in seminary. Nevertheless, he had contacts and friends. None who could help Emilia, of course. That he also knew. Still, it was up to Stefano to dictate what path he must travel to try to aid Emilia. He would cross the Bacino di San Marco to the mainland and meet Stefano in the late afternoon.

The current was in their favor and they were drawing up to the dock of the island just as the bell from the campanile, *La Nona*, marked midday. One of the monks had just put down his gardening tools to prepare to enter the church for the midday prayers. He hurried over to help them secure their small boat. "Fra Paolo is expecting you. He is overseeing the construction on the new library and should be heading to the church any moment." Lorenzo followed the young monk.

Pasqualigo hung back and began to pack a pipe to enjoy before he entered the Refectory. He heard the solemn minors of the Gregorian chant coming from the church. It sounded eerie to him, like the cry of a coot that had lost its mate in the marshes. He took a deep swallow from the flask of sweet wine and water that he had shared with the priest on the journey. He wondered what wonderful wine would accompany the lunch served in the Refectory by the brothers who grew and prepared all their foods, wines, honeys and liqueurs from the bounty of the island. He tried to identify the unease he felt, and decided to call it hunger.

In the narthex of the church, Paolo approached Lorenzo, shook his hand and kissed him on each cheek. "My old friend! It is so good to see you and to welcome you to our island of sanctuary. I have prepared a place for you in the Dormitory."

Lorenzo was moved by the warmth of the greeting. "Thank you so much, dear Paolo, for extending your hospitality to me. Staying here with you and your brethren will help me face the battle and the outcome of this sad affair."

Lorenzo paused and continued with a lighter tone, "It has been too long since the last time I visited and I am looking forward to whatever you have in store. You must tell me about the new library. Is it going as well as expected?"

"Lorenzo, pray for me! It is as though I have been thrown into a lion's den to prove my faith!" Fra Paolo shook his head solemnly. "But more later, after prayers and lunch. Come."

The simple fare of fave bean soup, boiled chicory, small fried fish, brown bread and flasks of light white wine was followed by sweet plums from the trees in the orchard behind the cloisters. Paolo and Lorenzo excused themselves promptly from the table where the other brothers lingered in quiet conversation. Don Lorenzo helped Pasqualigo back to the narrow dock and thanked him again for his help. He gave him his blessing for a safe trip back to Chioggia and pushed the boat clear of the quay.

Fra Paolo told of the problems with the construction of the library. The designs by Longhena, a young Venetian architect, were inspirational. Paolo showed Lorenzo the drawings of all the carved figures being crafted to adorn the grand room. "The main problem is getting the workers to stay on the task. There are constant stoppages and bribes are sometimes required to oil the wheels of progress on the thing." Paulo sighed. "It is a constant balance of diplomacy, tyranny and begging."

Their walk took them behind the cloisters to the quieter gardens and orchards. Small roughly hewn benches offered shade under the olive trees. "Tell me more about what has happened, Lorenzo. Rumours have flown from Venice, but one never knows how much is truth, fantasy or slander."

Don Lorenzo tried to organize his thoughts. Where to begin? "My sweet Emilia went to Cyprus with her husband, and to accompany the new bride, daughter of one of the Doge's favourites, Brabantio. It seems the girl eloped the night before with the renowned General Othello. Meanwhile, the Doge and the Council had demanded that the navy intervene to intercept a fleet of Turkish galleys off the coast of that island," the Priest paused for a moment in thought. "Why the Council permitted women to follow the Venetian Navy into what could have been a battle, is the first puzzle in this affair," he continued. "Emilia's boat travelled through a terrific storm, apparently; but she grew up with sailors and fisherman, the capricious sea all around her and I know that the tempest would not have caused her to become hysterical or confused. It seems that they arrived safely. The Turkish threat was quashed as much from the tempest as from the strategy of the *great* Othello," his voice was laced with bitterness, "and, in the week that followed, intrigues and treason from within the Venetian company ended with Brabantio's young daughter murdered, Othello taking his own life, and Emilia being stabbed by her husband, who was accused of treason, questioned and hanged in the government enclave on Cyprus." He took a deep breath and turned earnestly toward Paolo.

"I thank God that Emilia's wound was not fatal; but she was transported to Venice and is on trial for treason. Honestly, Paolo, I cannot imagine that she had any part in a plot against the state. She barely knew Desdemona and had only gone on the journey to accompany the young girl who insisted on being allowed to follow her husband. It is said that because of the elopement, her father washed his hands of her." Lorenzo dropped his head into his hands.

"All is confusion. The idea of a trial seems absurd. Emilia is not duplicitous. She has always been a child of Christ. A good daughter, wife and mother." He looked deeply into Brother Paolo's eyes, "Things are not as they should be. I must get to the bottom of it."

Brother Paolo placed his hand firmly on Lorenzo's shoulder. "I know you will help her with all that is in your power. The final outcome is, of course, in God's hands. I will ask the brethren to offer their evening matins for this cause."

"Thank you, dear friend. I know you are right. But it is so difficult to watch my sweet, pure child be used in this way, as a lesson from the State. She is innocent. I know she is innocent."

Now Lorenzo was to go to Venice, meet with Stefano, and try to be of assistance. He could hardly bring himself to think it, but really all that was left for him to do was to administer the last rites to the child he baptized, absolved, confirmed, married and counselled. If it came to pass, he would spend her last days with her. It had been her father's wish.

Lorenzo would have gone to her side anyway. As her confessor, it was his duty. As her "other father" it was his desire.

Chapter Five

$\mathcal{E}$milia had finally been able to approach Andrea for news of Dario just before he had boarded the ferry to Burano. He mentioned casually that in the autumn Dario was going to be apprenticed to the largest and most powerful guild in Venice: the *marangoni*, the guild of the carpenters. He had always been artistic and wanted to use his hands to build and create and with this appointment he would be offered many opportunities. Every art and craft and trade in Venice was erected into a guild. Although the government approval was necessary for the validity of the guild's charter, guilds were self-supporting, self-governing bodies. These groups were encouraged by the State, which used them as an outlet for the political activities of the people. Each new Doge entertained the guilds, who displayed specimens of their handiwork in the ducal palace. Guilds were called upon to partake in the pageantry when distinguished guests visited Venice. However, in Venice, unlike in other Italian towns, the guilds did not have a voice in the government of the State. This was not a concern, as most aristocrats in Venice were themselves members of a trade guild. Being part of this prestigious membership, Dario would find a patron to support him through commissions.

Emilia couldn't tell if she felt relieved or lost at the news of Dario's apprenticeship. Would she ever even see him again? She could feign some reason to visit Stefano in the autumn and perhaps he would help her find Dario. She held on to this fantasy on the dreamy voyage back to Chioggia.

"Emilia, Don Lorenzo and your father are in the salon and want to talk to you." Her mother's voice sounded solemn and gentle. Emilia searched her conscience for some sin she might have committed. She always felt a little guilty, even when she was completely in the state of grace.

It had been six months since the trip to Venice for Stefano's wedding. Her brother had not been back to Chioggia since the wedding; with Stefano in Venice, her father could be in Chioggia with them more. Emilia was soon to learn, however, that Vittorio's increasing presence in the home, diverted much of her mother's time and attention. Emilia missed having her mother all to herself, and now she felt even more lonely for Stefano. Everything was miserable, as far as Emilia was concerned. Even the important news that her father shared with them in September, that Maria Giustiana was to have a child in the late spring, did not console her. Again, she was confused by her feelings at this revelation. She felt jealous of all the loyalties that were pulling Stefano away from her. She had to share him with Giustiana, the business, and now, a child.

"You will become an aunt, Emilia," was her mother's comment, noting her daughter's frown at the news. But this hardly cheered her; Emilia's aunts in Burano were too old and serious for her to see any benefit in that position. Emilia recognized a selfish tendency in herself and felt ashamed. With a deep sigh she descended the narrow wooden staircase and entered the salon.

"God bless you, my child," Don Lorenzo placed his hand on her head and made the sign of the cross with his right hand over her. He is such a good man, Emilia thought. His goodness was like an aura that she entered whenever he was near. She turned to her father.

"Sit down, my daughter." He seemed almost a stranger to her. She had hoped that he would love her, but she could never seem to feel that love. It was understood, but not proved.

"As you know, we have been examining young men who have brought suit for the treasure of the Famiglia Baseggio, our darling daughter." Her father puffed himself with pride at his treasure and this made Emilia feel proud, too. She was his treasure. She was of value. But the word "suit" caused alarm and a tightening in her chest. She was almost fourteen and she knew that it was expected that she be married the following year. She had completely put the idea out of her head and now it was here - so soon.

"A particular young man has come to our attention. He is an Ensign in the service to the Republic and has brought honor to that position. He is from Asiago in the Veneto, so he is of the region. His family is a good one, respected and successful. He is twenty-two, which is the right age for him to consider taking a wife and beginning a family. There is only one dark spot on this golden horizon..." her father's voice trailed off.

Don Lorenzo jumped into the space left by her father's ponderings, "Because he is a man of the Doge's service, my dear, he must often go to sea and engage in battles. His life is full of danger, Our Lord preserve him. That is the only *caveat* on this match."

Her father came out of his meditation, "Yes, that is the worry, my child. He will be away at sea much of the time. It is arranged, therefore, that you can stay here with us when he is at sea. When he is in his home port of Venice, you will be with him there. It seems a bit upsetting, no? What do you think, child?" Emilia was amazed and speechless. Was her father actually asking her opinion? A sort of tenderness shone through his stern visage; it touched her.

"My father, I am in accordance with all of your wishes. I follow your decisions, as these are my duty and my heart. I want only to please you and bring honor to the family." It seemed the longest speech she had ever made to him. Don Lorenzo beamed at her as if to say, "*Brava*, Emilia, you have spoken well."

Her father beckoned her to him, "Come to me, my daughter. You are such an angel. So beautiful and obedient. I am so blessed with you and I thank God in my prayers every day that he sent you to us." He held her close. Emilia quietly wept at this shower of praise and approval. She wanted to melt into his arms and feel the safety of them forever.

Stepping back, her released her. There were some small tears in the corner of his eyes, but he had already composed himself. "It is settled," he said emphatically. He turned to leave the house and Don Lorenzo followed. Over his shoulder Vittorio said, "You and your mother will travel to Venice to meet with the young man in Stefano's house. I trust your brother to represent the family in offering the dowry."

Emilia had overheard her uncles discussing the dowry brought from Giustiana's family to her marriage with Stefano. She knew that the dowry was a way to show power and to curry favour with a powerful family. The father of the bride usually contributed one thousand ducats to the dowry, the additional amounts being contributed by other relatives. This enabled the dowry to exceed the limits put on dowries by laws drafted in the Senate more than a hundred years ago, dictating that the marriage settlement could be no more than sixteen hundred ducats. Fines were levied on husbands who received more than that amount from the bride's family.

The other stipulation written into the dowry contract was restitution of the dowry if the wife outlived her husband. Since many women did outlive their older husbands, this seemed fair in order for widows to be maintained. Then there was the matter of the *corredo*, which was a special marriage conveyance outside of the conventions that defined the dowry. In this way certain families could circumvent the limits set by the law. But the wise Senate had deemed the law necessary as more and more families were unable to raise a high enough dowry to find suitable husbands for their daughters. This in turn forced the families to turn over their unmarriageable daughters to the convent. Overall it was the fear of being dishonoured by offering what might be considered a paltry amount that led fathers to offer generously. The dowry was publicly discussed and it was a matter of pride.

So, in early February, Emilia and her mother sailed on the cold north winds to Venice. It was the first time Emilia was to visit Stefano in his new home. She was very excited to see him and hoped she would have time alone with him to ask about his marriage and ask advice about her own. Stefano would be the one to introduce her to her fiancé, and she trusted him to consider the match carefully.

She had no illusions about the process. This man would be her husband and she his wife, his chattel. It was written. She only hoped he would be a kind man. Stefano would know. She would trust him to draw this stranger out and to plumb his character.

Faustina and Emilia had hardly exchanged a word on the journey. Her mother carried her pillow for lace making with her and busied herself with her needle. Emilia read a small volume that Don Lorenzo had given her that provided a history of Venetian naval engagements. It was dry reading and Emilia found the movement of the boat working against her will to stay awake. When they arrived at the quay things moved quickly. They were met by Stefano's gondola and it was a rapid journey up the Grand Canal to the smaller canal past the Rialto.

Venice was different in winter. It was grey and damp. High water caused the piazzas to flood from the grates. People walked on stilted shoes or on planks of wood suspended over the water. The chill of the wind was biting and the large palaces never seemed to warm up or dry out. Stefano's house was not as large as a palace, but it was large enough and positioned on a small canal, Rio di San Lio, off the larger Rio di San Marina.

Emilia and her mother rode the gondola right up to the gate and stepped out onto a stone platform which led to storage areas. Water from the canal lapped freely over the edge and seeped into their shoes as they disembarked from the gondola. A stone staircase led to a courtyard on the next level where the well was positioned in the centre.

Under the Republic the water supply of Venice was furnished by the storage of rain-water, supplemented by water brought from Brenta in boats. The well consisted of a closed basin with a water-tight stratum of clay at the bottom, upon which a slab of stone was laid; a circular shaft of radiating bricks laid in a permeable jointing material of clay and sand was then built. At some distance from the shaft, a square water-tight wall was built. The space between the wall and the shaft was filled in with sand, which was purified of all saline matter by repeated washings.

At ground-level perforated stones set in tile at the four corners of the basin admitted the rain-water, which was discharged from the roofs by lead pipes; this water filtered through the sand and percolated into the shaft of the well where it could be drawn in copper buckets. The household sewage was discharged through pipes directly or indirectly into the canals. The rise and fall of the tide flushed the discharge pipes; it appeared that the native flora in the canals acted as a natural purifier to render this sluicing of waste harmless.

At the far end of the courtyard was another wide stone staircase, leading to the first floor, the *piano nobile.* Here the main hall was divided in to three areas which consisted of two corner rooms at the buildings front and a large central room. Heated with large fire places, each of these areas had a specific purpose: one served as a sitting room, one was a receiving room and the last served as a dining hall. Behind this the kitchens were located, and above these, rear staircases made of wood to allowed the cooks and servants to pass easily to the upper apartments.

On the next level was a library, a ballroom and, on one side, a wing that comprised the master's bedroom, dressing rooms and apartments. Further up a narrower staircase were the guest apartments. Emilia and her mother were shown into a comfortable set of rooms in that area. In their sitting room a fire was burning brightly and two soft chairs draped with lap rugs were pulled up to the grate. A servant carried in a tray of hot mulled wine and sweet biscuits.

"The Signora will be here shortly to greet you. She is resting." The man left them and closed the door softly.

Now, Emilia felt nervous. She was anxious to see Stefano, somewhat curious to see Giustiana, whom she had not seen since the wedding, and somewhat dreading the day, later in the week when she would meet her future husband.

The fire warmed and soothed them. Emilia felt drugged and fragile. Faustina started to pick up her lacework, but looked over at Emilia's pale face.

"Dear one, don't be afraid. Things have a way of turning out for the best and turning out well. You are a woman now and the ways of a woman and a wife will come very naturally to you. This man from Asiago will be blessed to have you care for him. Your bread is the tastiest, your pasta the lightest, your sauces the most fragrant. And more, you are beautiful, lively and giving."

"Furthermore," and her mother's voice took on a conspiratorial edge, "I was considering the plan for you to stay with us for periods when your husband is away at sea, and, Emilia, my heart fills with happiness when I know that you will not be taken away from us completely. What would I have done if your new husband came from a region far from here? It has been very hard for us to be apart from Stefano all these months and I am pleased that it will not be the case with our daughter."

All the while, Faustina was stroking Emilia's dark wavy hair and this caused tears to flow down Emilia's cheeks. She could not explain why, but tears flowed and flowed. "Darling, don't cry. Tell, mamma, what is troubling you."

"If I could put it into words, mamma, I would, because I know that you would understand and have a solution. I can't explain anything. I just feel so sad and so confused. I know I am a woman, but I want to be a girl. I am not ready to be grown up. I want to be your little girl again." She put her head in Faustina's lap and soon Faustina felt her throat constrict and tears begin to fill her own eyes.

"You will always be my little girl. My lovely little beautiful child. Always."

At that moment, there was a soft knock on the door. "May I enter?" Giustiana peeped around the door into the room. "Gracious heavens, what has happened?" Giustiana saw the tears on both their faces and was alarmed, fearing that someone in the family was ill or worse. "Please. Tell me!"

Faustina and Emilia leapt up at once and ran to Giustina. "It is nothing, dear. Only a tender moment with my little girl who is soon to be a wife." Faustina was somewhat embarrassed that they had presented such a tragic scene. Emilia was again struck by the beauty of the young woman. The blooms in her cheeks, the sheen of her hair seemed all the more vibrant with the evidence of the baby growing inside her.

"How are you, sister?" Giustiana embraced Emilia kissing her on each cheek and holding her away to look at her.

"I am well and I am very pleased to become an aunt! Surely you have stepped out of a fresco on a palace wall, so beautiful and delicate in your confinement. Indeed, it is so wonderful to have a sister!" She hugged Giustiana tightly.

"Come down and we will wait for Stefano. He should be here soon to share supper with us. The business keeps him very occupied, but we share this meal every night, no matter what pressing events try to drag him off." Giustiana was laughing and smiling. She seemed radiantly happy. "So this," Emilia thought, "is what it is like to be a wife. To be loved."

"Listen, Emilia, tomorrow I have my tailor coming to show me some fabrics. Would you like to have some dresses made in Venetian style? In fact, I was hoping to keep you here for Carnival. It is coming soon and you must stay to see the pageant. It is magnificent. Venice seems to show all of her charms and her tricks at that time. Can you stay? Please say you will!" Emilia looked beseechingly at her mother, who merely nodded and smiled widely. She would go back to Chioggia on her own. In fact, she was hoping that Emilia would feel that she could spend more time in this city, as it would soon be her home.

At that moment, Stefano came into the salon and Emilia ran to him, almost knocking him over with her exuberant hugs and kisses. His cloak was cold and damp with the winter mist of the canal.

"My little sparrow is growing into a lovely swan, a lovely black swan!" He kissed the top of her dark curls, " I have missed you, *carina*, more than you can know. It is so good to have you here with us now. Soon you will be our neighbour!"

She beamed at that thought. Her mother came forward and kissed both his cheeks. She wiped away more tears as he joked with her, telling her she looked even younger and lovelier than he had remembered. He promised not to let such a long time pass again before they were together. "You will be a grandmother soon and there are grave responsibilities to assume," he teased. He elicited a smile with his light-hearted joking.

When Emilia was able to look at him closely over dinner, Stefano looked tired and older. The business was draining him, perhaps. Or maybe it was the responsibility of the wife and baby weighing on him, she thought. When she mentioned it to her mother later, Faustina said, "It is the bitter cold of Venice that is taking all the blood from his face." Emilia understood that her mother yearned to have Stefano back in Chioggia where she could feed him, watch over him and protect him from the stresses of this big city.

After dinner the family sat before the large fireplace in the salon sipping glasses of warm sweet wine. Soon Maria Giustiana excused herself. With her confinement she had to sleep more and so they said good night to her. Stefano kissed her warmly on the mouth and held her swollen belly in his hands tenderly. Clearly they shared a deep love.

Stefano told Emilia and her mother that the day after tomorrow was set for a meeting with the bridegroom. Stefano had already met with Francesco Gradenigo several times and had received his family from the Veneto to discuss the dowry. He agreed with his father that the match would suit. Stefano felt comfortable about Francesco and trusted Emilia to bring dignity and honour to the meeting and the contract. However, it was still hard for him to imagine his little sparrow being grown and ready for marriage.

"His family," Stefano explained, "has long been identified with the parish of San Giovanni Evangelista de capite Rialto, and has a long and illustrious history in Venice. In the past they actively managed property in and near Chioggia. On the lido of Pellestrina they own over ten plots of cultivated land, fishing areas, and vineyards. They used to have saltpans, when that industry thrived. So as you can see, the workings and interests of our families are closely alligned. Now the Gradenigo family stay in the Veneto, in Asiago, and collect respectable portions of wine and fish from their holdings. In addition, they are involved in cloth trade with Florentine markets and this is a concern that we would like to explore."

Stefano stood and readjusted the logs and embers in the fireplace; he moved to replenish his mother's glass with more wine, but she placed her hand over the top so he poured a dram in Emilia's glass. She felt a little light-headed, but that could be the warmth of the fire close to her face and the cool draught at her back in the large room. The whole explanation about the Gradenigo family seemed removed from her, as if she were listening in to a conversation about someone else.

"The young man himself," Stefano continued, resettling in his chair, "seems a lively and popular gentlemen with his shipmates. I made inquiries and his General views him as invaluable to the crew for his honesty, loyalty and his initiative. Apparently he forms a strong bridge between the General and the ranks. What is more, he is young looking for his years and well-shaped." Emilia's fire-flushed cheeks burned even brighter when Stefano looked pointedly at her with this comment.

"My son," Faustina spoke for the first time, "I am so proud of you in your work here in Venice and I am completely comfortable that you have made a thorough study of this betrothal. Thank you, darling, for your devotion to us and to Emilia." She rose and sat next to her son. "We have missed you so much these months, but all news from Venice is in praise of your industry and acumen."

"Mamma, any praise I have earned is due to your and Pappa's guidance and attention. Come, you two have had a long journey. Let us retire now and tomorrow I can take you to my offices, if you like, or perhaps you would like to visit San Marco or the loggia and look at the beautiful glass wares of Venice. Let me know, whatever you wish." He led her to the stairs. Emilia followed them to the apartment. She held her brother one more time murmuring, "Sweet dreams, Stefano."

The next day Emilia and her mother had breakfast in a small sunroom off of their bedroom. Maria Giustiana was due to receive the tailor at eleven and Emilia was curious to see his textiles and to spend time with Giustiana. Faustina was going to meet Stefano close to that same time at a café near the Rialto and he would take her around the city. Her mother would return to the house for lunch and repose.

Emilia was still wearing the simple costume of Chioggia. Her dark cloak and skirt were made of a heavier woollen fabric for winter, but her blouse and shawl were the ones she always wore and were edged with the beautiful delicate lace of her mother's needle.

The Venetian dress was far more complicated and even simple daywear was fashioned of fine cloth, with many folds and layers; the gowns were adorned with delicate and rich embellishments of fringes, tassels and buttons. The outer cloak had a deep hood and was of fine wool mixed with silk that gave it a lightness but still provided warmth enough for the winds blowing up and down the canals.

The hair styles in Venice were also more intricate and clearly reflected influence from France. Even the men took pains to keep their hair in place and pulled back into a small band to fall down the back of the neck. Everyone looked courtly – even the guildsmen. Maria Giustiana's hooded cloak was edged in a thick ruff of soft mahogany fur; she tucked her hands into a generous muff of the same pelt.

Emilia was waiting in the salon as Giustiana entered; her maid took her cloak and muff and some small packages she carried. Giustiana had gone early to Ca' Foscari to visit her mother. There were many plans to make for the baby. Emilia thought how lucky her sister-in-law was to live in the same city as her parents.

At the appointed time, the servant led the tailor into the salon and he was followed by two workers laden with bolts of fabric and great wooden boxes of trims, designs and samples. The tailor was a serious gentleman in a dark, fitted suit. The buckles on his shoes seemed to shine like gold and his stockings were pristine white, despite the wet and muddy surface of every stone in Venice. He laid out his cloth on a long table that had been moved into the centre of the salon from against the wall where it had served as a sideboard. Each bolt of fabric was more exquisite than the one preceding it.

Emilia's head swam with the intricate strangeness of the designs, colours and textures. These fabrics came from Constantinople, Asia Minor, Egypt, and Flanders. There were brocades, damask, faille, silk moiré, Egyptian cotton with colourful embroidery, Flanders lace that was even more delicate than that from Burano. The shimmering colours of woven silks were as iridescent as butterfly wings or a beetle's carapace. There were layers and layers of textiles. How could one decide? Moreover, how could one imagine the dress or drape when looking at the waves of fabric on a table? Maria Giustiana seemed conversant in the sartorial language and asked about bias and selvage and weight or heft. Soon the tailor was making marks in his book to list her choices for various garments made of specific fabrics. She turned to Emilia.

"And for you, sister? What has caught your eye?"

Emilia felt completely bewildered. Having worn the simple cambric skirt and now the white linen half skirt over the dark wools all her life, she had no idea of how to begin to ask or tell. "Maria Giustiana, can you choose for me, please? I respect your taste and you have beautiful gowns."

The tailor turned to Giustiana, "Signora, allow me. May I suggest for the young signorina?" He pulled an emerald damask from the pile of bolts and held it up to Emilia's face. "How lovely!" he exclaimed. "With your complexion, this colour is magnificent, no?" he turned for Giustiana's opinion.

"It is perfect," she agreed. "Can you measure my sister for a fitted gown in the classic style? We will trust the trims and details to your expertise, Signor," She turned back to Emilia, "It really is magnificent with your beautiful skin and eyes. You resemble Stefano in many ways, Emilia. This gown will be beautiful on you and it will be my first gift for your trousseau."

Then Giustiana ordered some slips and blouses for Emilia in the Egyptian cottons and some sheeting in the same fabric for the baby's linen. The tailor agreed to come in three days for a fitting and to have the things ready in a week after that. It was settled and he left to return to his workshop.

The two young women retired to Giustiana's apartment where she excitedly showed Emilia the place for the baby's cradle in their room and the small room nearby for the wet nurse. All of the details of the decoration were delicate and subtle. Giustiana explained that they had changed the colours to the most soothing and calming colours for the infant. Emilia wondered how Giustiana would be able to contain her excitement until May.

That night, after another family dinner, Emilia lay awake for a long time listening to the wind that always seems to blow up and down the canals. Their apartments were too far above the water to be able to hear it lapping against the stones, but still she felt as if she were on a tremendous boat floating on a foreign sea to some new destiny. Suddenly her previous life in Chioggia seemed very long ago.

Chapter Six

"May I present my mother, Signora Baseggio. And this, mother, is Francesco Battista Gradenigo." The young man stepped forward and brought Faustina's extended hand up toward his lips as he made a shallow bow, removing his hat, a tricornered affair with the lion crest of San Marco on the crown. He moved the heels of his polished leather boots together. His dark blue serge uniform was resplendent with brass buttons, braid, and trim. "I am pleased to make your acquaintance, Signora."

He looked very elegant and it seemed obvious that he had tried to tame his curly black hair with a pomade to keep it from falling over his forehead. When he rose up, Faustina's eyes met his and she looked deeply into the dark blueness of them for a sign of goodness or treachery. He seemed completely at ease and met her gaze evenly. Satisfied, she lowered her eyes and he stepped back next to Stefano.

"My son has told me quite a bit about your family and your own reputation in the Doge's service. It is impressive," she smiled formally.

"My success with the Navy has been partly due to my fine General and the responsibilities he has seen fit to give me. We have fought many battles together and following his lead, I have done well and brought honour to Venice." His voice had a rich timbre, low and melodic. He spoke with a slight Venetian accent. There was a sparkle of playfulness in his eyes, despite the serious nature of the interview. Faustina felt that could be evidence of a fine wit and of a man who was not too vain to laugh at himself.

Stefano spoke next. "Francesco, I will ask my sister to join us. New and unschooled in the intrigues and styles of this great city, Venice, she is truly a young woman who is natural and domestic - *rubate all 'agricoltura*, stolen from the fields. She is the treasure of Chioggia and I know you will treat her as such. I believe you will form a blessed partnership."

Francesco smiled and made another small bow. Stefano signalled to the servant and he opened a door to the salon. Emilia had been listening to all of this from behind the door and her cheeks were burning with Stefano's last speech. How could he embarrass her so?

She lowered her eyes and carefully walked into the room and to her mother's side. Francesco came forward and took her hand to his lips, bowing as he had done for her mother. When she looked up, she was so surprised that she could not hide it from her face. Her mouth fell open and her eyes were wide. Francesco looked a little puzzled and concerned. "Signorina, I hope your first sight of me has not caused such dismay," he smiled gently hoping to put her at ease.

"But Signor, this is not my first sight of you! I recognize you from last summer on the *Ponte de Pugni,* where you were victorious!" She allowed herself to smile and made a small curtsy. His hand went involuntarily to his cheek which still bore an angry red scar from his wound.

"I am sure that if I had known of your presence, I would have fought all the harder and dedicated my small victory to you." He smiled in return slightly clicking his heels.

Stefano and Faustina were perplexed by this exchange. Neither had an inkling of Andrea's small crime in allowing Emilia to witness the spectacle. But since it seemed to help smooth what could have been an awkward meeting, they were more relieved than concerned that the two had somehow met previously, though not formally.

Francesco stayed for luncheon. There was lively conversation at the table about his family's business, the Baseggio business and the various escapades of the Navy. Francesco told them that he had allowed himself to be impressed into the service, but was pleased to leave an apprenticeship with a Venetian law office. His father had hoped he would go into the family business like his older brother had, but Francesco had demurred and was sent to Venice to study with a respected *avogadori*, law officer of the State. Philosophy and law had held an interest, but he had dreamed of the life outside of the courts and council rooms.

After 1545 Venice had recourse to conscription and it was not considered dishonourable to be drawn into service in this way. Because of his education and his family, even at the young age of thirteen, Francesco was given over to the General to be his cabin boy. He had been given more and more responsibility and was raised to Ensign by the time he was nineteen. His talent for logic and strategy, which had led his father to suggest the law, was appreciated in his role as Ensign. It was clear that he thoroughly enjoyed his vocation to service.

Francesco mentioned that he was due to leave the city with his ship and would be away for several months, and for that reason he offered to come the next day to walk with Emilia and Giustiana around Venice. His proposal was deemed appropriate and thus it was agreed that he could call for them in the morning.

Meanwhile, Stefano sent word to his father that the meeting went very well and that the arrangements for the wedding would proceed. Don Lorenzo would dictate the date for the union, which would take place in Chioggia in late summer.

That night, when Emilia was alone with her mother, she felt light hearted and a bit foolish for all of her confusion and sadness before. She told Faustina that she felt comfortable with this young man and was sure that they would get on together. Faustina was guardedly pleased; whether they got on or not was irrelevant, since the match had been set. Nevertheless, she had hoped her daughter would find the young man acceptable.

The next morning, Emilia knew that she truly looked like Stephano's little sparrow next to Maria Giustiana, who wore a simple dark grey dress, but still seemed to epitomize the elegance of Venice. Still, Emilia was proud of her origins on Chioggia and was pleased that her costume marked her as a native of that bustling and important island. The streets of Venice itself were teeming with exotic looking foreigners and it seemed that variety was the norm. When they stepped out of the gondola, Francesco took her arm and put it through his, taking Giustiana's arm on his other side. Although Giustiana had spent her whole life in Venice, she let him lead them and speak about the various sites they paused to view.

First he led them to San Stefano and the three made a brief visit to light a candle in the church dedicated to Stefano's name saint. Emilia was awed by the stately church and its lofty belltower. Francesco mentioned that this tower had been rebuilt; it collapsed after being struck by a lightening bolt that was so powerful that the bells had melted. Inside Francesco pointed out the ceiling which he proudly stated had been designed and fashioned by shipbuilders and thus resembled the inverted hull of a ship. The party left the church and wandered into a very narrow street. The narrowness caused Giustiana to laugh a bit at her awkwardness and Emilia laughed as well at their predicament. Francesco helped them through in his courtly way and made apologies for choosing this route, but clearly the young women found it amusing and were not at all perturbed.

They wandered in the Campo Sant'Angelo and ended in front of the impressive Scala del Bovolo, a spiral staircase encased in a tower. Then it was time to stop for refreshment and Giustiana suggested a café in the nearby Campo San Luca. Emilia and Giustiana ordered a hot chocolate drink, to warm them and a plate of *baicoli*, the flat sweet biscuit shaped like a butterfly. Francesco drank a small, strong coffee that had been "corrected" with a dram of brandy. Despite the brilliant sun, the February chill had reached their bones.

Next they walked to the Frati Minori Church where Giustiana wanted to show a sculpture of her ancestor, Doge Francesco Foscari. Afterward, as it was getting late, Giustiana suggested they head toward home, and Francesco decided to go by way of the Piazza San Marco. He pointed out the Piazzetta where executions took place between the two columns.

"The most notorious execution was that of the ambassador to Venice from France," Francesco casually reported. "He was flayed and hung by one leg for suspected espionage. Oddly, it was discovered later that the charges had been fabricated by his enemies and the man had, in fact, been innocent." Giustiana crossed herself at this morbid piece of history and they entered the Basilica.

Every time that Emilia stepped into this magnificent church she was struck all over again by the luminescence of the golden walls and ceiling fashioned out of thousands and thousands of tiny *tesserae*, squares of golden glass. On closer inspection the figures and stories of the mosaics began to emerge. It seemed impossible to note every image or masterpiece and she finally focused her eye on the altarpiece, the *Pala doro*, which resembled an icon made of solid gold encrusted with thousands of precious colourful gems depicting the Archangel Michael framed by scenes from the New Testament. The women lit candles and whispered personal prayers while Francesco stood at a distance, also awed by the magnificence of this sanctuary.

Despite the constant threats and battles with the Turks, this church seemed to express a humanistic side of the eastern nature. The altarpiece was fashioned in Constantinople and reminded him of other treasures he had seen on a visit to that majestic and embattled city with his General. Emilia looked back at him and sensed an impatience in his stance. Perhaps they had taken up enough of his time. She caught Giustiana's eye and signalled that they should go.

These days on dry ground had caused Francesco to feel an anxiety and impatience to be back on board the ship performing the duties that he found most satisfying. He yearned for the comraderie and the horseplay that was part of the fellowship of sailors. He had performed his duty to the Famiglia Baseggio and fulfilled his part of the contract; now he was itching to get back to the job of being an Ensign.

As they left the basilica, the midday bells began to toll from the belltower, so they boarded a gondola which carried them along the Rio di San Salvador across the Rio di Fave where it spills into the small Rio di Lio. At the landing of Casa Bassegio, Francesco bowed his head to Giustiana and thanked her for joining them on their tour around the city. Then he turned to Emilia, bowed deeply and kissed her hand. He looked into her eyes, "Emilia, I will be thinking of you on my long voyage, anxious to return."

"Safe journey, Francesco" she replied and smiled broadly at him. He left them on the landing and strode toward Strada Nuova and the Rialto Bridge.

Chapter Seven

When Lorenzo disembarked at the quay of Bacino San Marco, his eye travelled up the walls of the Doge's Palace. But he knew that the prison windows faced the back, if, indeed, Emilia's cell *had* a window. It was early yet for his appointment with Stefano, so he took the opportunity to step into the Basilica. He genuflected in the atrium, passed through Capella Zen, and paused to consider the baptistery where he had been present for the baptism of Vittorio, Stefano's son, seven years ago. He could not bear to go further into the church, crossed himself and left. Sitting at a small table in the Piazza with a café, he tried to compose himself.

"I am getting old," he thought. "Too old. I am no longer resilient and trusting in God's will." The pestilence that had returned to Venice and the surrounding area had taken Maria Giustiana and her small son five years ago. Don Lorenzo had felt inadequate in his office to console Stefano in this loss. Stefano harboured a lasting guilt for surviving the illness and sending his beautiful wife and baby ahead of him to the everlasting. Stefano felt himself doomed to live on. Eventually he refused to see the priest or receive the sacraments.

The priest looked up to the majestic domes of the Basilica. His spirit no longer soared at the sight. The powers of the saints, the church, and the Doge were useless against God's scourge. Almost fifteen years had passed since Venice had been brought to its knees. At times, Lorenzo, himself, wondered why he had been spared. Many in Chioggia had succumbed and he had been at their sides, anointing, giving final absolution, or holding the damp hand of death in his. The church had become wealthy in the desperate donations and offerings for masses, novenas, and even the undertaking of the building of another great church to celebrate - "Could that be the word?" he thought with disgust - the end of the plague.

Now Lorenzo thought that the vow to erect the new basilica seemed like a bargaining ploy that degraded prayer and faith. The designs for the church, itself, smacked of hubris. "Of course, the Venetians believed that the trial was over and that they had been saved, but the pestilence still came as predictably as the *aqua alta*," he thought. "Illness, death, destruction, these are always with us." He swallowed the last bitter dregs from his coffee and rose from the table. It was time.

The offices of Baseggio and Son were located near the Campo San Martino on the top floors of a modest building in the Castello, the shipbuilders' district, off the Fondamenta di Fronte. The building itself had slender columns at the entry, twin balconies on the first floor were supported by stylized bronze sea horses and there was perforated stone tracery above the windows. Inside there was a warren of smaller offices filled with clerks and clients, all of whom had a share in the profits and the successes of Baseggio's ventures. Father Lorenzo knew that branching into the cloth trade had been lucrative for the family and had overshadowed much of the earlier investments in fish, oil and trade galleys.

Stefano came into the entryway and held his hand out to Don Lorenzo. Lorenzo took his hand and pulled Stefano to him, kissing him on each cheek. He felt Stefano's body relax and even collapse a bit. It was tragic that this present concern is what finally brought

Stefano to call on the priest. It felt as though it came down to these two men to stand up for Emilia.

"Let us go up to my office, dear friend. I cannot tell you how much it means to me that you came and so quickly." Stefano had aged. His hair had turned mostly white and his skin looked taut and grey. His once lively eyes seemed sunken and empty. His shoulders were slumped and his muscular frame looked almost wasted. He turned and climbed the stone staircase with effort.

"I am pleased you felt you could call on me, Stefano. Now I pray that I can be of some assistance in clearing Emilia's name and bringing her home. Martina is on Burano with her grandmother and great aunts. She is too young to understand why her mamma is not with her."

The staircase wound up to another floor and the view from the windows was spectacular. The rooftops, campanile, domes and pinnacles spread like a confection to the west and the sun angled across the tiles causing them to reflect golden. The blue Adriatic sky seemed gaudy and mocking to Lorenzo's present mood.

Stefano sat behind a massive wooden table that was piled with charts, scrolls, and leather bound record books. It seemed to take tremendous effort for him to begin to speak. He took a deep breath and let it out in a sigh.

"I have had some trusted colleagues making inquiries on what course we can take to help Emilia's case. She is due to go before the Council in two days. Her lawyer, Dottore Santacroce, is visiting the prison every day, but my sister is still too ill to be of much help in filling in the facts of the events. She passes in and out of consciousness. On the other hand, I have discovered that we can place petitions in the Bocca di Leoni around the city." Stefano poured them each a dram of wine from a carafe on his desk and continued.

"As you know, the Supreme Tribunal is comprised of three inquisitors. Working on information from informers, they take part in intrigue and counter-espionage. Because the events in Cyprus occurred during a war action and there were attempts on the life of several officers of the Doge's service, one of whom died, the whole affair is seen as a possible case of treason, espionage or, at the very least, a mutiny. We have already passed the point where the Council of Ten, including *ex officio* the Doge and his six Councillors, have considered and ruled the case worthy of investigation and prosecution," Stefano swallowed the rest of his wine.

"In addition, as in all grave offences, the *Zonta* was called in, a number of prominent citizens who may or may not be consulted. There were several denunciations, one signed by Brabantio, which was expected, and two anonymous letters. A four-fifths vote of agreement was reached and the case has been added to the current agenda. Because the two denunciations were secret, the Doge and Council are bound to take it up and to decide if the matter of the accusation is of public concern. Being a possible case of treason, that issue was agreed upon." Stefano paused again. He had spoken all of this in a passionless, mechanical way. He stood up and began to pace the room.

"The warrant for her arrest was issued even before it was clear that she would survive her attack. Now it is up to Santacroce to disprove the charge," he dropped his voice.

"In the case of Francesco," he waved his hand impatiently, "Iago - the crime was committed outside of Venice, but within the competence of the Ten. Therefore, they delegated to the local magistrates in Cyprus, who held the trial and executed him on the Venetian enclave. Unfortunately, he refused to speak or shed any light on the affair, even under torture. It is all too amazing!" Once more he sank into his leather chair, exhausted by the effort of his report, but continuing.

"Of course, if we lose the suit, the sentence will certainly be that which is always handed down in cases of treason, hanging between the columns of the Piazzetta," he almost choked on this last phrase and his eyes slowly closed as his hands formed trembling fists.

"Dear Stefano, no. Do not even consider this. Emilia must be exonerated. At the very least she can plead incapacity. But I think that the truth will surface and that it will be proven that she has completely unaware of any intrigue." Lorenzo rose and stood behind Stefano, placing both of his hands on Stefano's shoulders. It was the first human contact that Stefano had known in almost five years and released the tension holding him together. His shoulders shook softly as he wept. The fists relaxed and he covered his face with his hands. The despair he felt was palpable and seemed to encompass more than the present tragedy.

"Will we be permitted to see her?" Lorenzo put his hopes into words. Stefano was not ready or able to answer and the question hung in the air like the motes of dust in the rays of the western sun setting beyond the rooftops.

When Don Lorenzo left the offices, he walked aimlessly for what seemed hours. Finally he came out of his trance and found himself wading through the end of the day bustle of Rialto Bridge. He knew that he was expected back at San Giorgio for evening prayers, but he did not feel ready to pass by the Palace and cross the Basin yet. Instead he wanted to lose himself in the solitude of the throng of money-changers, bankers and money lenders along the Canal. The human tide was always surging one way or another across the bridge, and he allowed himself to be carried along to the far side, where he continued his journey in a trance.

Lorenzo walked through the *Merceria* and found himself outside San Zulian; he paused only a moment before he turned back and recrossed the bridge. He had counted on the emptiness of the fish market at this hour, and it seemed to suit. He slipped into a small café near the vacant, yet fragrant stalls. It somehow reminded him of Chioggia and he felt soothed.

Chapter Eight

*E*milia opened her eyes. The light was dim and she was alone. There were muffled sounds of wind, water, distant bells; but these were signs she recognized as night sounds. The wooden floors that had been installed as an improvement in the Piombi, had provided a comfortable nesting place for the cockroaches that scratched their nightly journeys to and fro. In the wood multitudes of fleas lived, procreated, fed and died. Emilia was trying to ascertain if the annoyance of their bites was new or if she had only recovered enough now to notice the itching and scabs on her legs and under her hair.

The nurse had helped her, she recalled, in the last days or could it have been weeks, when the pressure or urgency of urination had caused discomfort. Now she felt strong enough that she might navigate her way to the enamel bowl in the corner of the room – slowly – but independently. The effort of throwing back the light coverlet caused her arms to feel leaden and weak. As she swung her legs over the side of the cot, they felt as if they did not belong to her and a tingling sensation signalled a return of the blood to her feet. She made a brief inventory of her upper body and gently patted her side where the knife had entered, passed close to, but had not pierced, her liver or spleen. The movement and touch caused no pain. In fact, her whole side felt numb.

Emilia used the wall along the right side of the cell to balance her slow and tentative steps toward the corner. The cockroaches scuttled out of her way, surprised at this new invasion, being used to free passage all the night and most of the daylight hours. A watery moon reflected off the ceramic plate that covered the bowl. Emilia pushed the plate aside and it clattered to the floor. The insects that had been trapped or chosen to occupy the rank vessel scurried over the edge. They were filthy and Emilia shuddered involuntarily as one scrambled over her foot in its rush to move away from the disturbance.

Lifting her thin skirts she squatted over the bowl as best she could. Her body swayed and she gripped the rough wall with her fingernails. It was as though the evacuation had to be willed. She concentrated and soon a warm stream trickled into the bowl and she felt some relief. Emilia lowered her skirt and started to rise and stand. She felt light-headed and the dizziness increased until she could no longer balance against the wall and slid to the wooden floor, knocking the bowl to its side. She was aware of a ringing – the bells, what did they mean?

"Those bells are calling us to the Piazzetta. The pageant is beginning. Quickly. Emilia, put on your mask and cape," Giustiana was wearing an ivory satin gown with deep long sleeves edged in black. Her cape was the reverse and her mask was white papier mache with white and black plumes framing the top and thin red paint on the mouth. On one cheek was an exaggerated beauty mark and she held a decorated fan open at her chin. She was standing before a long mounted, ormolu mirror admiring the effect of her costume. Stefano entered with a flourish in a traditional tricornered black hat trimmed a long willowy plume, the traditional white mask, and a black cape.

"Principessa, may I escort you?" he made a deep bow to his wife. To Emilia they looked like elegant illustrations from the Tarot – The King and Queen of Batons.

"And my adorable sister, you look lovely, too," he helped her into her black cape which did not completely cover the emerald green gown that had been prepared by the artful tailor. The bodice was very low, which was the style in Venice. In fact, some of the women copied the French fashion and almost completely exposed their bosom. The edge of the bodice and along the shoulders was trimmed with a lacy ruching of the same fabric sown with tiny glass beads of gold. The same beading decorated the front of the gown and spilled down the skirt all the way to the bottom, which had at least four centimetres of the pattern circling the hem. Her shoes were black leather with double bows of the green damask at each toe. She held a gold fan, beaded to match the pattern on the dress.

Emilia wore a powdered wig and a narrow mask that only covered her eyes, so Giustiana had dusted a fine flour over her face and throat and coloured her lips with red wax. The whole effect was transforming. Emilia thought there was something very liberating about dressing in a costume. She could be anyone or anything she wished for that night.

Even the gondolier was in a mask and cape. The whole city was enjoying the Carnival. No one chose to recall the history of the masks, used when the pestilence had visited the region. Now it was donned to celebrate and Emilia was fascinated by the variations, extravagance, and whimsy of the many costumed people crushing into the Piazza in front of the Basilica. The opening of the festival was marked by an acrobat posing as a pirate who slid down wires and ropes from the top of the campanile to the loggia in front of the Doge's Palace. Stefano was hovering protectively near his wife, aware that the crush of people could be upsetting to her in her condition. Her gown ingeniously disguised her growing belly, but she instinctively had one hand over it, as a buffer against the seething crowd.

The bells continued ringing almost discordantly and heralds blew the signal from the second balcony of the Palace. A collective sigh went up as the acrobat appeared in the top arches of the bell tower and prepared his descent. It happened quickly, but still, to Emilia, it was as if time were slowed. She adjusted her mask to centre her eyes over the holes in it. She wanted to see every detail. Cape flowing, hat held with one hand and mask in place, the "Turk" floated down the almost invisible cables. The sword in his scabbard flashed in the torchlight as he landed on two feet and sprung around as if to challenge the spectators, who all sent up a tumultuous cheer. "Let the festivities start!"

As the three threaded through the crowded alleyways and small squares, strangers greeted them; everyone seemed a stranger in a mask. It was inevitable, but not necessarily worrisome, that they might be separated. Stefano had reassured himself that Emilia knew the way back to the house if they did lose each other. He stayed very close to Giustiana, carefully guiding her through the stream of masked revellers.

Stopping in awe to view the colourful costumes and incredible masks, soon Emilia had lost sight of her brother and sister-in-law in the crush. Around one corner she thought she recognized Stefano, but, of course, the majority of men wore the white mask, thricornered hat and cape, so the men she approached never ended up being Stefano and she had to excuse herself and move on.

The tenor of the festival was one whereby everyone was interested in playing practical jokes, being mistaken for someone else, or perhaps teasing a young signorina into taking off her mask. This seemed to be the case when a group of three masked young men were making a show of detaining every unaccompanied young woman along the calle. They bowled up to Emilia and in the Venetian dialect challenged her to guess their names. The most aggressive one wore the *maschera de becca* that had a long phallic nose protruding out of a deep dusky red mask. Rather than the tricornered hat, he wore a sort of pointed clown hat and was dressed entirely in black, even down to his stockings. His compatriots were dressed more traditionally, although one wore a mask that only covered his eyes.

Emilia could not understand the rough dialect and felt a bit threatened by the long nosed boy. Finally she removed her mask to try to entreat them to let her pass. The two masked fellows, laughed loudly at their success and bowed deeply to her. The one with the half mask noticed tears in the young girl's eyes and recognized something in her accent. He, too, removed his mask and looked closely at her. When she raised her eyes she felt she would swoon.

"Emilia! It is I, Dario," he exclaimed with surprise.

"Oh, Dario," she fell against him with relief and amazement. He took her by the shoulders and held her as if to prove to himself that she was not an illusion.

"What are you doing here, dear one?" He hugged her to himself and whispered, "I never thought I would see you again and now you are here in Venice." He turned to his laughing friends, who were enjoying the whole scene even more than if she had been a random stranger they had harassed with their pranks. Dario seemed a bit angry and embarrassed at his friends' behaviour.

"Caravello! Enough! The joke is done. Go on without me, I have met an old dear family friend and must deliver her safely to her lodging."

This statement only caused a greater roar of merriment. "*Si*, of course, my friend. You do that. Take the young lady to safety. We will carry on our promenade without you and hope to find 'old dear family friends' of our own, eh, Franco?" Caravello winked at his laughing partner.

"That's right! Dario. Wish us some of your good luck, *Ciao*," they passed on into the throng and Dario put his arm protectively around Emilia's shoulder.

"Come. We can find a café on the other side of the next bridge that may be quieter than these streets so near San Marco." He led her carefully through the narrow street against the current of the tide of revellers. It seemed that the streets automatically reverted to passages going one direction only and the pair had to find the parallel street to go back the other way. Soon they passed over a quiet bridge near the Fenice Theatre and moving several streets west, they paused on the edge of the Grand Canal downstream from the Rialto and away from the crowds. They entered a small café that was full, but the *barista* signalled for them to go toward the back where a small table meant for one was removed enough from the noise to enable conversation. Dario pulled up another chair next to Emilia's, which placed her tightly between himself and the wall – out of harm's way. A carafe of white wine appeared on the table and Dario ordered the traditional Carnival pancakes, *fritole*.

"I have been staying with Stefano and his wife Giustiana since February and they encouraged me to remain to experience the pageant Now I am particularly glad that I accepted their invitation." She looked at him adoringly. He had not changed at all and it was as if a year and a half had not passed since they had been floating and kissing on the waterways in Burano.

"I came to Venice myself last September. I have been working with the carpenters guild and it has been magnificent. Oh, Emilia, I would never have imagined how much there is to learn about wood and its properties. Each tree yields a different magic or utility. Because I have shown a delicate touch, I am being trained to create figures out of wood, decorative pieces which may adorn an altar or form a monument; but, in addition, I have learned how to use the grain of the wood to find the strongest parts to be used for beams or planks." He showed her his hands and she gasped. The once delicate soft palms were scored with scars and layered with callouses. They were the hands of a labourer, not an artisan. He sensed her thoughts.

"Yes, these used to be the hands that could unfasten the small hooks on your bodice without you even noticing – and all that in a rocking boat, as you might recall," he smiled that smile that had made her feel like they would never be apart. "It is nothing, my sweet, I can still manage!" He broke into a broader smile and laughed gently.

Emilia knew that she had more news to share, but could not bring herself to end this tender moment. It would end soon enough and she had forced herself to put Dario out of her mind long ago. And yet, it was as Stefano had said: She was Dario's and he was hers. That would never change. Dario was looking closely at her. The dusting of flour had been brushed away in places to reveal the olive smoothness of her skin. She held the white wig in her lap and her dark hair had escaped into a tangle of curls. Her mouth was what he had remembered so clearly – it was full and soft and easy to smile. Her eyes were dark and liquid like a strong café. Tonight they seemed even deeper and harder to read.

"You are tired. Can I escort you back to Casa Baseggio? We apprentices have been given several days rest to prepare for Lent and I could come for you tomorrow. We could have a whole day together. Will you be in Venice much longer? I want all the news from Chioggia."

"I *am* a little weary," Emilia was not so much tired as feeling sad. "I would like very much to have you walk me home, Dario. About tomorrow, I will have to see. Perhaps you could tell me where I might find you in late morning, if I can slip away." Already Emilia was feeling the sin behind her plan. She was succumbing to a temptation, she knew. But, on the other hand, they were good friends, and it would not be dishonest or disloyal to meet and talk. She was convincing herself with this rationalization, but she knew that she could not let Giustiana or Stefano know of her assignation, if indeed, it did take place.

Dario left some coins on the table and led her out into the street. If anything, it seemed more crowded rather than less in the later hour. She did not know the names of all the streets, but instinctively knew the way back to Rio di Lio. They paused under the covered walkway. Dario was holding her around her waist and rhymically squeezing her to him almost absentmindedly as he tried to decide the best way out of the crowds. Then he suggested they hire a gondola knowing that the waterways would provide an easier exit than the narrow, clogged streets.

Finally he led her to a boat landing and waved to the gondolier who was lounging on the quay. He had raised his mask to eat the fried dough strips dusted with sugar. When he saw Dario's signal, he tossed the last bit of dough into the canal, and readjusted his mask as he stepped into his boat. The shiny black lacquer of the boat's hull reflected again the reflections in the water of the many torches that lined the streets festively. Dario got into the boat first without letting go of Emilia's hand. He spoke quickly to the gondolier and handed him some coins. The curved, sabre-toothed decoration on the prow of the boat eased up past the slippery stair that would allow Emilia to step into the gondola. As Dario lifted her over the side, her gown caught on a splintered piling and a tearing sound caused her to tighten almost overbalancing the two of them. With a laugh, Dario quickly whipped the gown away from the rough wood as the gondolier moved his oar in the forked oarlock and they pushed from the landing stage into the centre of the canal.

Dario carefully led her to the cushions under a tapestry canopy, which provided protection in wet weather, but also privacy. Emilia let herself be lowered down to the roughly upholstered cushions. They had been covered with pieces of woven carpeting in rich Persian designs. It reminded her of a picture she had seen in a book about the Sultan's harem. Dario stretched out beside her and took her chin in his hands. She knew what was coming and surrendered to his eager kisses.

She did not give thought to the time that had passed, but later understood that Dario must have paid the gondolier to travel the most circuitous waterways to Rio di Lio. Dario had been honest when he said he could still caress gently despite his hardened hands. The open bodice of her dress made it even simpler for him to pass under the heavy fabric and hold her breast. Her heart fluttered like a captured dove beneath the gentle weight of his hand's exploration. His kisses were more ardent and urgent than they had been in Burano. They were no longer children exploring. They were two lovers intent on experiencing all the pleasures, or nearly all, under the chill of the starry night. The gondolier kept his eyes above the level of the fringed canopy. He was not unused to lovers using his boat for their stolen moments. He liked to imagine the sculpted bronze seahorses that formed cleats on either side of the gondola as emblematic of his nighttime role of purveyor of love. By day he merely transported people. At night they were transported by their amorous caresses in the cradle of his boat.

Stefano was awake and alert when Emilia finally stepped into the hallway. He rushed toward her and held her arms.

"Emilia, I was worried sick. I had visions of you falling into a canal or becoming lost and afraid in the labyrinth of streets." He hugged her tightly. He had removed his costume and wore a loose dressing gown of grey velvet and black velvet slippers. Clearly the rest of the household were in bed.

"I am so sorry, brother. I was carried beyond you by the revellers and a miracle occurred. Just when I began to feel completely lost, I was found." She had decided to share a certain amount of the truth about this evening.

"Emilia, you speak in riddles. Please, tell me," his relief was quickly turning to annoyance now that he knew she was safe.

"Dearest, I am sorry. What I want to say is that I met Dario Saranzo from Burano in the street! He is in Venice as an apprentice and it was such an odd coincidence that tonight, of all nights, we would find and recognize each other. He took me to a café for pancakes and wine and we caught up with all the news of our lives. Then he escorted me home" She clutched her cape around her, unsure of how dishevelled she might appear. It was late and the excitement of the whole evening was giving way to exhaustion. "Let us retire, Stefano. I am so sorry to cause you concern. It is true. I did have a brief moment of panic when I realized that we had become separated and that it would be impossible to find you, but it all turned out well."

She kissed him lightly on his cheeks and he took her arm as far as the staircase.

"Emilia, I am happy that you had a chance to reunite with Dario and I know how much his friendship means to you. But remember, *cara*, you have been promised. Friendship is all that may pass between you now," the gentleness in his voice did not mask the seriousness of his admonition.

Emilia felt her cheeks burn with the shame of knowing that she had betrayed her promise tonight. She decided that she would meet Dario the next day and explain to him that they would treasure their friendship and let their passion pass into the memory of the night of masquerade and magic. If she could not do that, she would surely be doomed to bring dishonour to her family and pain to the one she loved.

Chapter Nine

*E*milia did not meet with Dario the next day as they had appointed.

Instead, she took an early ferry back to Chioggia; she would spend Lent and Easter with her mother and help with the preparations for her wedding, which was set for the second Sunday in July. At that time Stefano and Giustiana's baby would be old enough to travel or to leave in the care of the nurse. Moreover, that date would not interfere with the feast of Il Redentore, which was the feast held to celebrate the dedication of the Church of the Redemption, built as a thanks offering to God for the end of the plague in 1576 by Doge Mocenigo. The celebration involved a solemn procession over a bridge of boats across the Canale della Giudecca followed by an incredible pyrotechnic display from barges positioned in the canal.

Many of Vittorio's clients from Venice would be invited to Chioggia to celebrate the wedding and it would be awkward to ask Venetians to come away from their city on the third Sunday of July.

The forty days of Lent marked a time of fasting and abstaining from meat, but it was meant also to be a time of reflection and rededication to Christ. Emilia took part in the weekly way of the Cross, the vigils and the masses led by Don Lorenzo, but she felt false to this show of dedication. Don Lorenzo noticed that Emilia had not come to him to give her confession in the whole of the Lenten time and had not taken communion at the masses. To him this could mean only one thing: that Emilia was not in the state of grace and had not yet felt the contrition necessary to make a good confession.

In the last week leading up to the Resurrection and the Easter Vigil, he decided to approach her. It was the duty of every Catholic to give confession and receive Holy Communion during the Easter period.

Emilia had come to San Domenico to help prepare for the Passion Week services. The altar boys had taken care of the candles, the incense, the palanquin, which would be used to carry the image of crucified

Christ, and the banners. Emilia and her mother had been charged to wash, mend and press the linens used in all the services. Her mother had trimmed the altar clothes and various napkins used in the lavabo of the mass with her fine lace. She taught Emilia the formula of mild soap and lemon juice used in the delicate washing that would remove all traces of the wine that might have spotted the linens. Don Lorenzo would bless the washing water, as the drops wine had been changed into the blood of Christ. Emilia found the whole process soothing and was pleased to be part of Don Lorenzo's services.

"Emilia, my child, I am concerned about you," Lorenzo broached the subject that had been weighing heavily on his mind through the Lenten period as they were sorting the linens together in the long shallow drawers of the armadio that was lined with thin sheets of paper and sprigs of lavender and laurel to discourage insects.

"But why, Father? I am fine. It is good to be here in Chioggia helping my mother. It is peaceful here and uncomplicated." She knew exactly what the priest was moving toward, but hoped to divert or at least delay the conference.

"Emilia, look at me. I am your Patrinus. You can tell me anything that is on your mind. You are my

118

precious child and the precious child of Christ. Don't turn from us, especially in a time of trial," he held her chin and had turned to look deeply into her eyes.

She gently pulled away. "I am simply preparing myself for the big step in my life that is coming soon. It is a step that I was destined to make, but over which I have had little control. I hope that I am ready and that I can accept the role." She closed the topic, sliding the drawer of the armadio shut. She turned away from the task and reached for her shawl.

"There. Everything is in place. We are ready for Holy Week." She felt his eyes upon her, probing, and turned to face him, "Patrinus, of course I know that you are only trying to help me. I promise I will come to you when I need advice."

"Yes, Emilia. And will you perform your Easter Duty in the next week?" he called after her as she was heading out the side door of the Sacristy.

"Yes, of course," she replied over her shoulder. He shook his head slowly. He knew her too well to accept this answer. There was something – something more. In spite of her obedience and dedication to all that was demanded from her by her family and her Lord, Emilia had a stubbornness, a wilfulness which had developed into a cynicism that would help her as an adult in the city of Venice; still, it made him sad to recognize the necessity of such an innocent to become wise in the ways of the adult world. It was inevitable, but he felt a sense of loss.

By the time late April had arrived, the plans for the wedding were suspended in anticipation of birth of Stefano and Giustiana's baby. Emilia and her mother arrived in Venice several days before the celebration of the Patron Saint of the city. The festival commemorated April 25th, the day upon which, it is said, the body of Saint Mark was spirited out of Alexandria in a cargo of pork. Because of the Muslim abhorrence of that meat, the shipment was not carefully inspected by the custom officials and therefore arrived safely in Venice, the city evangelized by St. Mark.

The other tradition associated with April 25th was the gift of a rosebud to a woman as a love pledge. The legend associated with this tradition involved the star-crossed love of Tancredi, a troubadour, for Maria Participazio, a noblewoman. Tancredi joined the army hoping to be praised for his valor which might enable him to reach a level worthy of Maria's hand in marriage. However, in serving as a valiant soldier in the war of Charles the Great against the Arabians in Spain, he received a fatal wound and fell into a rose bush that turned red with his blood.

Tancredi's dying wish was for his paladin, Orlando, to deliver a blossom from the bush to his beloved Maria in Venice. Orlando reached Venice the day before the Patron Saint Day and delivered the bloom. The next day Maria was found dead holding the rose bud next to her heart. Thus began the Venetian tradition of giving the red rosebud to a beloved woman on St. Mark's Day.

When a rosebud, or *bocolo*, was delivered to Stefano's house for Emilia, everyone assumed that it had been sent from her betrothed, Francesco Gradenigo. But the message was cryptic. Faustina read it after Emilia had opened the ornate piece of paper that had been wound around the delicate stem of the rosebud, fully expecting to find a sweet message from her fiancé.

"What does it mean, Emilia?" she asked, frankly confused. Emilia blushed with embarrassment and consternation. The message was clear to her, but how could she explain that it was not a love pledge from Francesco, but a rosebud from Dario. The note read: "To my true lost love. We are forever bound by the unspoken vow of our passion."

Venice, although a large and prosperous city, was really a village. The narrow streets and the island mentality made it a place where there were no secrets. It was not difficult for Dario to learn that Emilia was in the city staying at Casa Baseggio. He had also learned of her betrothal and impending marriage. He would respect her privacy and accept the contract of her marriage. But since she had not met him that day back in February, he wanted the chance to at least bid her farewell. The *bocolo* was a perfect answer to his dilemma. He had not foreseen that any eyes save Emilia's would peruse his message.

"Mamma, it is from Dario Saranzo." Emilia braced herself for the storm she was sure would break over her head at this news.

"Ah," she looked resignedly at her daughter. "Stefano told me you had spent almost an entire night with Dario at Carnival. And your brother assured me that you had made your peace with the young man. Emilia, have you been corresponding with him?" her mother's voice sounded stern.

Emilia could not hold back the tears of shame, frustration and anger. She shouted defensively, "No! I have not spoken to him, met him or communicated with him since that night we shared. And I am all the more miserable for it!" she sobbed into her skirt. Dario cared for her, knew her, really *knew* her. They were friends. Instead she was to be bound for her life to a stranger chosen by her parents in a type of business contract. It seemed barbaric and she felt doomed.

"Compose yourself, Signorina!" Her mother crushed the note in her hand. "His name is never to be mentioned again. It is over, do you understand, Emilia? Over!" her mother's voice sounded hard and cruel, but also frightened.

"In as much as we have ever communicated, it *is* over, Mamma. But I will never stop loving him or he me. That is that!" she stormed out of the salon clutching her rosebud and almost knocking over the servant coming through with a tray of refreshments.

Early in May the midwife was summoned to Casa Baseggio. She and Faustina helped in the delivery of Giustiana's strong, squalling boy – Vittorio Alessandro. The midwife claimed that she had never assisted in an easier birth. Giustiana was calm and efficient in bringing her son into the world. Word was sent that Don Lorenzo would be welcomed to assist Giustiana's family priest in the Baptism. Emilia Baseggio and Francesco Gradenigo were to be named godparents to the child.

Vittorio Alessandro was a red and creamy baby whose eyes did not open for almost three days. When he finally chose to look at the world, he seemed pleased at what he saw, as his father could swear he detected a tiny smile on his son's lips. Giustiana did not have the heart to explain that this was a normal digestive response in young babies. She was simply thankful to present her dear husband with an heir.

The shock of straight black hair thinned and by the time he was to be baptized Vittorio's head was smooth with only soft brown fuzz. He had the delicate features of Giustiana and the watery hazel eyes of Stefano. On the back of his neck were some reddish marks, which the midwife had claimed were where the angels had kissed the child before his birth and were a sign of good fortune.

Vittorio Alessandro was to be baptized at San Marco and announcements were delivered to the many friends of both families. As the date approached, Emilia was ambivalent about seeing Francesco again. She had not been in his company since February when he had escorted her around the city. Her nervousness increased when he arrived the day before the baptism and shared supper with the family.

Francesco was tender with the baby and insisted on holding him briefly. "To practice for tomorrow," he claimed. His face seemed to glow as he looked down into the squirming baby's face. There was a connection between them that touched Emilia. This man was gentle and unafraid to show that gentleness. He was not hardened or proud.

He seemed reluctant to give the child back to the nurse, but then quickly rejoined the adults in conversation about Venice's political news. Her father was discussing the present Doge Francesco Erizzo. His predeccesor, Nicol Contarini had ruled Venice for only one year before succumbing to the plague that swept into Venice from Mantua.

Erizzo, had had to contend with serious issues. When the Duke of Mantua died, a power struggle ensued in northern Italy. Venice was allied with the French in an attempt to crush the Hapsburgs and Savoy, but peace was finally made without Venice being included in the treaty and Mantua was lost to the French. Plague was the result of the war and it moved from the mainland to Venice like a raging wildfire, decimating the population. At the end of a year and a half the plague finally ended and the first stone of Santa Maria della Salute was set in the foundation in thanks. Although the plague had ceased to fell masses of inhabitants of the city, there was always a danger lurking. Small outbreaks continued to occur.

The very mention of the plague caused the women to cross themselves and Giustiana asked that the women be excused to the salon for mild liqueurs. The men were left at the table with more fortified *grappe*.

Faustina hoped that becoming more familiar with her fiancé would settle Emilia and she suggested that the two betrothed retire to the smaller receiving room. Faustina reasoned that the family certainly did not need to witness any more petulant outbursts from Emilia; and her mother was convinced that the unpleasantness could be averted if only Emilia were given the opportunity to become more acquainted with the charming young officer.

Not daunted by the challenge of his reluctant betrothed, Francesco was able to carry on a lively conversation despite Emilia responding only in phrases. He enjoyed recounting the various comedies and victories of life on the seas. He explained the ever present dangers to Venice and the need for constant vigilance against the various enemies of the State, in particular, the Turks.

"Our galleys are on report for any emergency. When not out on the sea, we engage in war exercises on the decks and maintain strict discipline. But we play hard, too," Francesco's eyes sparkled with excitement when he talked about the galley and the men. "Our General is an excellent leader and under his command

I have learned much. I hope to rise up in the ranks with his recommendation."

Little by little, Emilia relaxed her guard and softened her resolve of not letting this young man win her friendship. She asked him why his shipmates addressed him as "Iago" rather than his given name of Francesco or even Gradenigo.

"There are three sailors named Francesco in our company and the confusion of always calling 'Francesco d'Asiago' caused the name to be shortened to 'Iago' using the last part of my village name – Asiago." He asked her about life in Chioggia and talked about his knowledge of the terrible War of Chioggia.

"In 1378 the Genoese admiral, Pierto Doria intended to make Chioggia his head-quarters and thus began a tug of war between the Venetian commander, Pisani, and Doria that lasted two years. The whole population of the island dug in their heels, despite famine and hardship, to help quash the Genoese. Chioggia is famous for its proud, determined citizens. The victorious outcome of this battle left the Republic of Venice the supreme naval Power. Genoa has never fully recovered!" crowed Francesco, "In great part, this victory is owed to the Chioggiotti." He looked deeply into her eyes, "Are you proud and determined, Emilia?"

"Of course. I am Chioggiotti!" Emilia put an aggressive expression on her face, but the smile in her eyes, betrayed her playful answer to his challenge.

"I am so glad to learn this, Emilia," he took her hand in his. Hers was soft and limp and his was strong and tanned by the sun. He turned hers over and kissed the palm. Emilia suppressed a shiver. "I admire determination and strength in a woman," he continued to hold her hand in his.

"My Patrinus gave me a book of the naval history of Venice and I have been studying all the engagements and victories. I would like to learn more," she gently extracted her hand and smoothed her skirt. "Would you like a café or other refreshment?"

"No. Thank you, dearest. May I address you thus?" he smiled engagingly. He was flirting with her. "I would like to discuss our responsibilities toward Vittorio Alessandro. It is a very great honour and I want to discharge my duties well."

"We, as his godparents, speak on his behalf tomorrow during the responsive part of the ritual. Our real duties will not begin until he is of the age of reason, Francesco." She was speaking matter-of-factly and trying not to put any softness in her voice. "It is an honour, and, as you say, a responsibility. I am sure we are up to it." She allowed herself to look into his eyes. They were so blue and vital that she found she was staring. "You are good with children. I noticed it when you held little Vittorio."

"I have two younger brothers. My mother entrusted them to me when she and the maids were busy with other duties. I welcomed their questions and willingness to let me dictate our games. They were apt pupils for learning all of the animals and plants in the nature of our region. Frankly, I miss them. My work takes me away so much, it will have been over a year when I see them in July at our marriage." Francesco seemed nostalgic for his life at home. "They will be so excited to meet you, and," he looked down at his hands, awkwardly, "perhaps we will give them some young nephews and nieces to teach, as I tried to teach them." He reached across and took both her hands in his. "I want so much to have a family, you see, Emilia."

This confession embarrassed Emilia, but she politely answered, "Family is important, I agree, Francesco." She stood up and he rose with her. "It is late. Shall we join the others, Francesco?" The tone of her voice was firm and seemed to say: the interview is over.

"As you wish, dearest."

After the ceremony in San Marco, a grand luncheon reception was given to celebrate the next heir to the Baseggio enterprises. Maria Giustiana looked radiant and she offered her young son to anyone who asked to hold him. He was wearing the same Baptismal gown that her husband had worn twenty-four years earlier and it was elegant fine linen embellished with rows of embroidery. The matching cap had long since been forsaken as the baby fussed to have it on and tied beneath his plump chin. He wore tiny linen boots with lace edging designed and executed by his grandmother, Faustina. Stefano stood between his wife and mother looking for all the world like the Duke, himself.

Over and over, the guests approached Emilia and Francesco commenting on what a beautiful couple they made. In a way, the event served to present them to the society of Venice and prepare the way for the celebration that would take place in under eight weeks.

Chapter Ten

The guard found her slumped on the floor when he opened the cell to give the prisoner her bread and warmed milk with coffee in the morning. He set down the tray on the narrow rough wood table and lifted her under her arms, dragging her as gently as he could, back to her pallet. She was aware of the movement and opened her eyes after he lowered her onto the cot. Her mouth felt dry and her eyes felt sandy.

"Thank you. I don't know what happened. I only remember trying to walk to the corner…"

"Signora, do not try to speak. The nurse is heating water to bathe you and we have clean clothes. It seems today you must go to the Council for a preliminary statement of some kind." He quietly left the cell, but did not close the door completely. The room smelled vile. He knew she was under arrest for treason, but somehow she did not seem any danger to the State in this condition.

The nurse had removed all of Emilia's clothes and left her standing with a clean sheet draped around her lower body. She was standing in a shallow basin of warm water and the nurse was using a large sea sponge to lather her body and then pour water over her from a pitcher.

"These rags will have to be burned, Madame," the nurse held the bundle at arms length. Several men came in to remove the mattress and replace it with a fresh bag of straw and wool. Emilia was too weak to even try to cover herself, and besides, what would be the point of a show of modesty? Another woman, with a kerchief wrapped around her head, was scrubbing the wooden floor with soapy water. Emilia looked down at herself. The wound below her ribs on the left side was a reddish purple scar that was shaped like a large fishhook.

What drew her notice were the silvery tracings of the marks that represented her motherhood. Her belly had grown large with a child. Her breasts hung limply and her skin sagged. It was the body of an under nourished crone rather than a young woman of twenty-one years. The nurse was scrubbing her head and lathering her hair with a strong smelling soap. The water ran down in brownish rivulets – the result of the scabbed fleabites opening and bleeding. The pain of the process felt strangely reassuring to Emilia. She had been without sensation for so many weeks. When the cleansing was over, she was dressed in her clothes from Chioggia. Stefano had brought a clean blouse, skirt and stockings from home. When her hair had dried somewhat and the nurse had brushed it and tied it up on top of her head, Emilia felt recovered and strong.

"Dottore Santacroce and your brother will come to take you to the Council Chamber. Only Santacroce will be allowed to go in to the Inquisitors with you, however," the nurse spoke without emotion as she put the finishing touches on Emilia's hair and straightened her collar. "There, you look presentable, Signora," she picked up the towels and sponges and left the room. Emilia sat on the edge of her cot and tried to collect her thoughts. What sorts of questions would they ask her?

A slight commotion in the hall drew her attention and no sooner had she looked up than she felt she was seeing a vision. Stefano ran to her side and lifted her gently into his arms. She felt warm tears on her neck as he sobbed to see her thus.

"My darling, darling sister. I have been so worried. You are safe now, and I will not let them harm you anymore. I will make sure you can come home with me. I am here. I will take care of you, my darling." He was almost incoherent in his emotional pledge. Emilia wanted to believe what he was saying, but she knew there was little likelihood that she would be able to simply leave this place and go home. There were charges to be answered and punishments to be meted out. That much she had come to understand, despite her lapses into unconsciousness.

"I am well, Stefano. I am well. Do not weep, my dear. It will be all right. Everything will be sorted out. Do not fear for me. Please, my sweet," she found herself trying to console him. She supposed it must have been a terrible trial to be the one watching her slow recovery from near death and wondering what had happened on the far island of Cyprus that had led to this scandal and imprisonment. She was relieved that he had not seen her several hours earlier in the state she had been in before the nurse had helped her bathe.

Stefano lowered her into the chair nearby and composed himself as the lawyer came into the cell. He had waited discreetly outside to allow privacy in this reunion between brother and sister.

"Well, Signora, you are looking much improved today. I am sure that you will make a good impression on the Council. Before we must go down, can you try to help me understand what happened on the island?"

Emilia thought she might need to begin at the beginning and relate how she happened to be included in the party, which sailed for Cyprus; but the real beginning was long before that fateful trip. It had really started almost six years earlier. It had started with the vows she made on her wedding morning; vows which bound her to Francesco. She had pledged to love, to honour, and to obey.

The whole town was festooned with carpets and tapestries hanging from the windows and balconies. Flowers bloomed in pots all along the street leading to the church and the steps were lined with pots of colourful geraniums and begonias. A cool sea breeze rustled the plane trees, olive and lemon trees in the piazza. Everything seemed fresh and fragrant despite the July heat. Her mother, her aunts and all the women of the island had been working in the weeks before to prepare the traditional dishes that would crown the celebration of Emilia's wedding.

The recipes had been handed down, reworked and polished as the tastes and ingredients had changed. With every new commodity, spice or aromatic herb that arrived on the exotic merchant galleys berthing first in Chioggia, the recipes would alter to become even more imaginative, fragrant and succulent. The subtle use of spices indicated status and prestige generated from the wealth of the Chioggian merchants who traded them.

A favourite spice in the Chioggian kitchen was clove and this was used to peak the taste in everything from panforte to fowls and lamb. Married with cinnamon, cardamom and coriander, the breasts of wild ducks from the marshes were a delicately perfumed and garnished with plums from the trees which grew in all the island squares. The other exotic spice, new to the Venetians, was saffron. The traditional ingredients of garlic, olive oil, parsley, oregano and basil would be suffused with a sauce made of sour grapes and saffron. The dish took on the hue of a monk's robes from

Asia, but the local grapes and white wine brought the Chioggian chicken back to the Adriatic.

Being an island, the many fruits of the sea were apparent in the feast. Baked red mullet with sage, sea bass poached in seasoned broth, bream grilled on great narrow spits and split into halves, mussels, clams and prawns in great bowls of pasta or in creamy risotto. Finally there were fat shiny stuffed squid, knotty salads of octopus and peppers and tiny fried fish.

There were oval plates of the famous red lettuce from Chioggia, *radicchio*, that had been grilled and bowls of grassy *agretti* with lemon and oil sprinkled over it. Boiled and seasoned chickory was curled like a nest around a paste made from dried fava bean. Deep bowls filled with baby artichokes were nestled next to shallow dishes of thick green olive oil. The artichokes were dipped in the oil and eaten raw. Golden pumpkins from the farms of the islands were used in recipes for crepes, pastas or simply sliced and grilled. Green sweet melon was sliced and used as edible garnish around the various fruit platters and meat dishes.

One of the precious imports of the time and region was the lemon. Oil from the skin was believed to be an antidote to the plague. The juice from a lemon could ease the pains of childbirth. The Venetians found symbolism in the perfumed flower, which flourished at the same time as the ripening of the fruit; this phenomenon was connected to the Mary's dual role as virgin and mother of Christ. In ancient festivals the potent shape of the lemon suggested fertility, one end representing a phallus, the other suggesting a nipple. The orthodox Jews believed that an infertile woman could conceive if she bit off and ate the flower end of the lemon. The lovely fruit was even seen as an antidote to the poison of a scorpion bite.

In the Chioggian kitchen the skins, juice and pulp of lemons were used in ices, puddings and sauces. They were preserved in syrup or used raw as a relish for the rich roasts or pickled. The golden, pungent slices garnished the meat and fish platters and added a piquant touch to the sauces.

Every one of the women had their own specialty, which they insisted be added to the table. The men, not to be outdone, rolled great rumbling barrels of their best wines and smaller casks of *grappe* to be included with the feast.

The day before the wedding, Francesco and his family arrived. Emilia met Francesco's mother, Signora Maddelena Martina Gradenigo and his father, Signore

Pietro Giovanni Gradenigo at the landing stage in the harbour of Chioggia. Emilia presented Signora Gradenigo with a bouquet of flowers and kissed her on both cheeks. She curtsied to his father; and Francesco, who was at his side, stepped up to Emilia and embraced her kissing her cheeks. He introduced his older brother Carlo, named for his grandfather, who looked as old as Stefano. And then he proudly introduced his two younger brothers, Sebastiano and Nicolo, who immediately initiated a playful wrestling match, pretending to throw Francesco in the water. They stopped reluctantly when they noticed their mother's raised eyebrow and skipped toward the campo behind the procession led by their parents and the betrothed.

That evening Don Lorenzo gave an offering over a light supper and the two families spoke amiably about Chioggia, Venice, business and family. Stefano and Giustiana held court with tiny Vittorio cooing and kicking as Sebastiano and Nicolo tickled him.

Emilia felt like a swimmer caught in a strong current: she relaxed and did not fight the pull of the event. She even found herself enjoying the attention. The most attentive was Francesco, who brought her dishes of food, held her arm when she rose from the chair, refreshed her wine glass and generally behaved like her valet. His activity on her behalf seemed to peak her own passiveness. She felt almost drugged and found it difficult to animate herself in conversation. Finally, the evening came to a close and the two families bid each other a good night with much kissing and hand shaking.

Her mother was helping her arrange her trousseau in the sturdy walnut trunk her father had given her. It had been his grandmother's chest and had a simple but evocative painting of Madonna and Child scene on the inside lid. It was laden with linens, undergarments, simple dresses, shawls, lacy dresser scarves and other fine articles that would help Emilia begin housekeeping in Venice.

Francesco's father had provided them with a lovely apartment that was the first floor of a former palace known as the Palazzo Mastelli del Cammello, named for the relief on one of the corner columns of the palace showing a man pulling a camel. Francesco explained that the building was alongside the Rio della Madonna dell'Orto, the jewel of the quiet square was the Church dedicated to the Madonna dell'Orto. Signora Gradenigo told Emilia that the apartment was very comfortable and dry. She had stayed there many times when she had reason to come to Venice.

"Emilia?" Her mother was carefully placing lavendar pillows in between the folds of pillow covers.

"Si, Mamma?" Emilia answered while she was taking down her hair and absentmindedly passing a brush through it.

"Are you prepared for tomorrow?" Her mother came over to her and stood behind her looking into Emilia's reflection in the mirror. "Have you become any easier about the marriage?" She tenderly took the brush from her daughter's hand and began to brush Emilia's long dark hair much as she had done when Emilia was a young child.

"I am fine, Mamma. Francesco is very kind and respectful to me. When I see him playing with his little brothers and speaking to his parents, I can tell that he is a good man. He will take good care of me and I will do my best to be a good wife to him." She turned and held her mother's hand, stopping the brush, "Mamma, you have shown me what it means to be a good wife and loving mother. I have your pattern to follow and I hope I can be as successful as you have been. I love you, Mamma. I am sorry if I have given you any reason to worry." Emilia stood and held her mother.

"I am so happy, Emilia. Yes, he is a good man and I know that tomorrow will not be a trial for you. You are more than ready to assume your place beside him. I pray that you will grow to love him as much as I have grown to love your father." Faustina paused as if trying to find words. "Emilia, I know we have talked about what our duty is to our husbands. Be patient with him and it will go easily for you."

Emilia smiled. "I have discussed the first night with my cousins and aunts, Mamma. I know what I must do. I will be fine." She hugged her mother tightly and then continued her preparation for bed. Neither woman felt she would be able to sleep with all the details and the anticipation of tomorrow's ritual.

Don Lorenzo offered the Mass and the sacrament of Holy Matrimony was incorporated into the service. Emilia had finally made her confession and been absolved for her temptation with Dario. She was ready to receive communion and to say the vows which would bind her forever to the man by her side. As they walked back down the aisle of the church and entered the square, a great cheer went up as the guests and all the townspeople applauded and small girls threw rose petals in their path.

Emilia was too excited and busy greeting guests to eat anything at the wedding banquet and finally Francesco led her to a waiting boat that would take them to Venice. It was under an almost full moon as they left the landing stage in Chioggia. Both mothers stood on the quay waving damp handkerchiefs as the rest of the guests continued to eat and toast the couple, happily waving them off and cheering for the groom to perform his duty well that night.

It was midnight when Francesco helped Emilia through the outer door of the apartment. Several men from the landing stage had followed with Emilia's trunk and other packages and chests sent by her family. Signora Gradenigo was accurate in saying that the apartment was dry and pleasant. Moonlight spilled through tall windows, which overlooked the canal and richly polished wood furniture glowed in the salon. At the back of the apartment the bedroom was furnished with a large curtained bed that was made up with embroidered sheets and many soft pillows. There was a dressing table and armadio on one side and a small settee in front of a fireplace on the other.

"Oh, Francesco, it is lovely. I think I shall be very happy here in my new home. Thank you," Emilia smiled and kissed his cheek.

"It is suitable, but eventually we will have to find a larger house, cara," he looked critically at the place. It had been improved and he knew his mother had gone to some trouble to make it comfortable for Emilia and himself. He felt extremely tired from the past days and wondered how he would prevent himself from falling asleep as soon as he lay his head on the pillow.

He left Emilia alone to prepare for bed and went to the kitchen to bring a carafe of water and some glasses to the bedroom. When he returned, Emilia was in bed with the light sheet pulled over her.

"Dearest, I already love you deeply, you know. I am sure you think it is impossible, but I knew it the first day we met at Stefano's house and you told me you had seen my little war of the cane." He was sitting on the edge of the bed smoothing the soft hairs from Emilia's forehead. "We have had such a long day, do you mind if I let you sleep and we can plan our day when we wake up tomorrow?"

"That would be lovely, Francesco. I, too, am tired and feel dull. Will you stay with me tonight?"

"Of course. Let me hang my clothes up and I will be right back." He left the room quietly. Next door was a dressing room with a day bed and a desk in it, that Emilia assumed was his small office. She closed her eyes and thought that this wedding night was perfect.

The next morning Emilia awoke as a maid knocked and entered the room. She had a tray with café, warm milk and bread. Another maid followed her with a basin of water and towels. Emilia's clothes had been unpacked and arranged in the armadio and in a small chest of drawers. Her brushes and combs were set out on the dressing table and her dressing gown was draped across the settee. She was uncertain if Francesco had slept beside her at all, since the bed seemed barely turned down. The two maids opened the shutters and the bright Venetian sun poured into the room, cheering it.

"Signora, I am Carolina and this is my sister Angelina. Our aunt works in Asiago with the Famiglia Gradenigo. The Signora has engaged us to help run the household. We can go to the market and prepare meals, if you wish. Also, we keep the apartment clean and do the laundry." The two were only slightly older than Emilia and it seemed strange to her to have servants. But, of course, she would need help since she was unfamiliar with Venice and with the ways of the Gradenigo family.

"How kind of Signora Gradenigo to arrange this for me. I am very pleased that you will be here to help me, Carolina and Angelina." The two sisters curtsied and went on with preparing water for Emilia's toilette.

"Signor Francesco went out early on business and asked me to tell you he would be back mid morning." Carolina seemed to be the spokesman of the two. They left her to dress and have her café. Emilia knew that Francesco was being thoughtful in giving her privacy for her first morning as his wife. She wondered if his mother had mentioned that a young wife might need some privacy or if he instinctively knew.

Emilia dressed in one of the simple Venetian gowns that Giustiana had helped her order from the tailor. Now that she was the Ensign's wife, she would try to comply with the style of Venice.

By midday Emilia had tired of waiting in the salon for Francesco to return. Carolina and Angelina had gone about their duties and had left to have their own lunch and repose. They would return at five o'clock to begin preparations for supper. Emilia felt a deep loneliness. She was a stranger in the city in a strange apartment. She didn't know if she should leave and wander a bit on her own, or continue to wait at home for her husband. She had enough coins to take a gondola to Stefano's house, but he and Giustiana had planned to stay through the week in Chioggia. She did not know a soul in Venice. But then, Emilia remembered that she *did* know someone. But, no, she would not allow herself to even acknowledge that thought. She was no longer Emilia Baseggio. She was the Ensign's wife.

By three in the afternoon, Emilia had explored the whole of the apartment. She had hesitated to go into Francesco's dressing room, but eventually included that area in her roaming. She found his desk with some books, journals, and his closet. She brushed her hand over the several uniforms that hung there and saw his boots and shoes arranged in neat rows.

In the kitchen she ate a piece of fruit and several slices of cheese. She had barely eaten anything in almost two days. She was far too excited to eat the day before the wedding and too busy at the wedding banquet itself. Emilia thought longingly of all the wonderful foods that she had helped prepare and had not tasted. She felt hungry and sorry for herself. She found some cider in the cold chest, and poured a generous amount in a delicate glass goblet she had discovered in a cupboard.

Finally, she went to the bedroom and took off her gown. She lay down on the pillows in her slip and fell into a deep sleep.

"Emilia? Dearest?" Francesco was gently rubbing her cheek. "Wake up, darling. I am so sorry I left for so long. I went to the ship and the sailors all wanted to toast my wedding and before I knew it, the day had almost passed." He was speaking softly in her ear. "Forgive me. I hope you were not worried or too bored here all alone."

"I must have dozed off." She tried to sit up. Francesco gently pushed her down on the pillows and he was lightly kissing her face and neck. "Francesco, no, please. I am not awake."

"But you are so beautiful when you are asleep. I was watching you for some minutes before I woke you. I cannot believe that you are mine. I am so lucky." He continued to stroke and kiss her neck. His hair smelled salty and slightly of wine.

"I told my sailors that I am the luckiest man alive." He eased onto the bed beside her.

He was wearing an open shirt like the one he had been wearing in the battle on the bridge. The small ties that close it were dangling and she could see the beginning of the dark hairs on his chest. She felt the strength of his arms through the thin muslin as he worked his arm under her and drew her to him. She liked being held in his strong embrace. His muscles were working to move her closer to him until the two were pressed together facing each other on their sides. His lips found her mouth and he kissed her deeply. His eyes were closed and Emilia noticed that there was a deep furrow between his brows, as if he were concentrating very hard on a problem.

"Emilia, my wife, my love," he sat up long enough to pull off his boots and unlace the front of his trousers. His shirt was pulled over his head and Emilia saw that the soft dark hairs spread across his chest in a heart shape and then trailed in a line down to the lacings of his pantaloon. His muscles tensed as he threw the shirt from the bed and the late afternoon light reflected off the sheen of the smooth dark skin of his back. He lay back down next to her and stroked her hair and neck once more. His eyes were so dark blue that they looked black in the shadow of the curtained bed.

"Don't be afraid, my darling. I will wait for you to say when you are ready to become my wife – my real wife." This must be the problem that creased his brow, she thought. She had gotten used to the stroking and kissing. She wanted it to continue.

"I am your wife and I am ready to share your life, and myself, with you, Francesco. We made our vows." To prove her words, she kissed him warmly on his face, on his eyes and then on his mouth.

His fingers opened the bodice of her slip and he kissed her breasts and held her hips with his hands. Emilia felt a warmth in her abdomen growing and her breath came in shallow gasps as he moved his hands under her slip and explored her body tenderly while kissing her mouth and breasts and neck. She felt weakness in her legs and a wetness between them.

Francesco carefully turned her away from him, so her back was toward him. Then she felt the warm firmness of him rubbing against the back of her thighs and working into the crevice below her buttocks. She felt a moment of panic, but before she could even call out, he had entered her and pushed deep inside her; he was holding her breasts tightly to pull her closer to him as he thrust against her. He kissed and gently nipped the back of her neck and moaned with each movement deeper into her.

The surprising thing to Emilia was that there was no pain; the women had described their first time with their husbands in language of war – it had torn and bled and they had felt wounded and violated. For Emilia it was none of these things. It seemed that Francesco had prepared the way with his hands and kisses so that she was *willing* him to penetrate her and take her. The sensations of the nerves in that place, that centre, were too complex to describe or understand. It felt full and tender and aching. She arched her back to meet his movement and he let out a deep sigh that seemed to come from his soul. And lay spent.

She *was* his wife.

Chapter Eleven

$\mathcal{T}$wo weeks passed before Francesco had to return to his ship and set off for Crete. He would be gone for a month. The first weekend after their marriage was the festival of The Redeemer and Stefano suggested the four of them celebrate the evening together. Giustiana took Emilia aside and asked her how she was enjoying married life and if she was comfortable in the apartment. She seemed pleased when Emilia described both aspects effusively.

"Francesco is a gentle and considerate husband and his parents have given us a lovely first home here in Venice. I hope you will come visit me soon. Francesco leaves in a week to sail to Crete and I will be alone for several months."

"August is a time to go to the Brenta Valley. Come with us to our villa there, Emilia. It would be lovely to be all together and Vittorio can become more acquainted with his aunt." Giustiana was insistent and they spent time that day planning all that they would do in August. Giustiana was anxious to learn some of Emilia's recipes and Emilia looked forward to spending time with her sweet nephew.

In the weeks before Francesco had to leave, Emilia spent her mornings following Carolina to the market and learning from the young native. They travelled to the Dordosuro Quarter, along Rio San Barnaba where gondolas laden with fruits and vegetables rocked next to the walkways along the canal. Emilia was introduced to the vendors who sold the freshest produce for recipes she hoped to prepare for her husband. Francesco had spoken of the rations of dried meat and hard bread on board the galley, and she was determined to make the table at home a feast of the most creative and succulent dishes she could prepare.

In the market near the Rialto Emilia recognized the vegetables and salads that had been brought to Venice from Chioggian gardens; there were wonderful leaves and herbs used to mix a tender slightly seasoned salad leaves called *mischianza*. Pyramids of fruits from the fertile mainland farms were stacked on long wooden planks. The top of each would be crowned with a piece, carved open to show the juicy interior.

She saw the turbaned women on low stools with their skirts tucked between their legs using a sharp knife to deftly cut away all the leaves and choke of the small artichokes; with a twist of the wrist it was done and the pale green "bottom" was dropped into a bucket of lemony water.

Deep vats of brine contained all the varieties of olives available: many shades of green, from almost deep brown to the palest leaf. The black olives had a variety of shapes and skins: some pointed on each end and tight skinned, others round as small melons or wrinkled like the cheeks of the crones hawking them. Some rested in a peppery oil and laurel "soup". Some were dry and heaped on burlap sacking.

There were tables of round wheels of hard cheese, vats of milky water in which buffalo cheese floated, and flat circles of runny soft goat cheeses and cheese wrapped and tied like a gift in palm leaves.

Further along were stalls of hanging meats: great dried legs from wild boar; fat hard columns of salami, and rashers of bacon, striped red and white with lean and fat like flags, and glistening delicacies of cheeks of boar. The bustle and noise were amazing and exciting.

Carolina bargained in the local Venetian dialect and Emilia stood by trying to take in the words and mark the reactions. They walked down the quay along the Grand Canal and crossed over the Rialto with the mobs of people out taking the view, or, as they were, searching for the best item around which to build a lunch.

The fish market was extensive, but Emilia had been spoiled by fish for sale on the dock at Chioggia. In fact, most of these fish had stopped first at her island and been sold on to the Venetian vendors. Nevertheless, there were plenty of varieties to tempt her. Emilia recalled the fish auctions on the docks at Chioggia, which were eerily silent conducted with elaborate hand signals. She had never witnessed such a frenetic display of bargaining, shouting, and shrill hawking as she saw in Venice.

Again, Carolina had particular sellers that knew her and she had built a rapport with them so that the bargaining was more playful than fierce. The women added paper wrappers of baby red mullet to their baskets of vegetables and dried meats. Emilia had started the dough for the thin crepe-like pasta, and planned to fill them simply with soft cow cheese and herbs. The fish would be fried as the second plate with bowls of tender salad leaves drizzled with the aromatic balsamic vinegar shipped from Modena to this market.

Carolina's sister, Angelina, had gone out early that morning for fresh bread and new wine. The cask at home was almost empty and Emilia had deigned the dregs useful only for cooking.

With the temptations of her kitchen, Emilia had persuaded Francesco to come home for his lunch and repose. It was a habit he was eager to form and he found the time at home was a welcome rest from the responsibilities on the ship. There were many preparations to be made before they sailed in a fortnight, but being newly married he allowed himself this midday break. Emilia fully understood her motive for bringing Francesco home for the midday meal and siesta; she had engineered these luncheon rendezvous only because she wanted him to make love to her.

After lunch they would stay at the table and talk about her morning, news from family, her plans in his absence. Soon Emilia would suggest they rest before he had to return to the ship and he would react as if it were a novel, but good idea. Then they would move to their bedroom, which had been shuttered from the midday sun and was coolly dim. They would take off their outer clothes and lie down in slips and linens. The pretence was that they would actually sleep for a time.

Lying next to him, Emilia liked to trace her fingers over Francesco's face. It was a beautiful face, she told him. She knew he was self-conscious about his scar, but she told him that it was dear to her because she had witnessed the battle whereby he had earned it. The scar would turn dark when he blushed or was excited; it was a barometer of his feelings. Emilia knew she could cause this change.

In fact, the power she had over him made her giddy. He would respond to her light touch and turn to her and want to kiss and hold her. Soon he could stand it no longer and would pull away her slip and take her. With time he had become bolder and a bit rougher with her. She met his urgency with her own and he was pleased.

"You are my fiery little animal. Who would have guessed that you would be so passionate? You are made for this, cara mia. You are generous with your favours and you make me mad with wanting you."

This thrilled Emilia. It was the love and devotion she had yearned for all of her life. She had understood so little before; now she had a secret knowledge that excited her more than even the pleasure of his body. With her kisses and caresses she could make this strong man as weak as a kitten; she could ensure that he would want her and love her always. When his face loomed over her as he rocked inside of her, she watched the concentration increase and his scar would grow darker. She closed her own eyes then, because she knew he would soon sigh his deep sigh and roll away from her exhausted with his labours. He loved her.

Chapter Twelve

Before Francesco left on the galley for Crete, he told Emilia that he was displeased with the plan for her to go to the Foscari Villa in the Brenta Valley. He had heard about the parties and the liberties taken on these hedonistic summers spent out of Venice and he did not want his wife to be part of the society there.

"The cavorting of the women and their lovers in the city was shocking enough," he thought as he tried to explain to Emilia his misgivings. He knew she admired her sister-in-law and worshipped her brother, but he would have to insist that Emilia spend her August in Chioggia with her mother.

"When your father interviewed me he was uneasy with the knowledge that I would be away sometimes for months at a time. It seemed to be a good solution for you to return to Chioggia in my absences, Emilia. The Venetian women are known for their licentious behaviour. It is common knowledge that Venetian wives define indiscretion as having *more* than one lover behind their husband's back. The very costume of the Venetian woman is almost indistinguishable from that of the courtesans who brazenly frequent the streets." His scar was becoming darker and darker at the vehemence of his argument.

"It is for this reason that I must *forbid* you to join Giustiana in August at the Villa." He stood with his arms crossed, waiting for her response.

Emilia was surprised at Francesco's demeanour. She had only seen gentle concern for her welfare and this ultimatum inspired her to resist. In fact, she did not really care either way whether she went to Brenta or went home for the two months of Francesco's duty aboard the ship. But on principle, she wanted to clarify that his demands were founded on an irrational belief that she was not trustworthy.

"Francesco, I would think that my passing time with family members would be acceptable to my husband, whether those family members are in Chioggia or Brenta or..or..." she tried to imagine the most outrageous option she could conjure,

"Constantinople for that matter!" She also crossed her arms. Her cheeks were burning and she was prepared to battle him on this point. She *was* trustworthy. She was *not* a Venetian courtesan. She was the Ensign's wife!

Francesco's arms dropped to his sides and his mouth opened. The fire in her blood, which seemed to excite him in their love making, was another thing altogether when he was instructing her on how to obey his wishes. But Francesco was a diplomat and in his dealings with recalcitrant sailors he knew that sometimes a softer approach would achieve the intended result. He reached out to her and she stiffened, but allowed him to hold her.

"Of course you are correct. Your family are honourable and you are without any guile. You are perfection, mia cara. Perfection!" He held her away from him to look into her eyes. She looked wary, but was softening.

"If you insist on going to the Brenta in August, of course you may. I only feel protective of you since you are innocent of the wiles of these Venetians. Also, I am selfish. I do not want any other young men to admire you. You are so beautiful, I am sure you will turn many heads. Some of these young nobles find it an interesting game to seduce young wives." She bristled again, so he quickly added, "But you are above reproach and I know you would comport yourself perfectly." He hugged her to himself and kissed her cheek tenderly.

"What it comes down to, Emilia, is that I am dreading being away from you at all. I have come to depend on you as my confidant and my support. Oh, how I will miss making love to you." He continued to hold her and felt her begin to respond to his caress.

"I, too, am dreading these months apart, darling. Of course, I will go to Chioggia. My mother will need me and I miss her. Rest easy, Francesco. I am yours and yours alone."

His ship left for Crete and Emilia excused herself from the Brenta excursion by pleading that her mother would welcome her home to help and keep her company.

"Perhaps another August, Giustiana. You are very generous to offer to include me in your holiday, but I must return to Chioggia."

Chapter Thirteen

August in Chioggia was pleasant for Emilia. There were moments when she forgot that she was married and no longer a resident of her island – she did not feel like a visitor. She fell into the routines that had been her girlhood joys: the kitchen, the garden, and sitting on the quay watching the harbour fill and empty. Unlike Venice where there were throngs of exotic strangers and the close-knit community of natives, neither of whom knew or particularly cared for Emilia, in Chioggia she was known and greeted by all. She was the daughter of Vittorio and Faustina, sister of Stefano and, now, the Ensign's wife. They had processed and celebrated at her wedding and welcomed her back for the lazy month with open arms.

She heard from her father of Stefano and Giustiana's August in Brenta and the grand festival of the return of the Venetians from their holiday in villas along the river. The first Sunday of September marked the majestic re-entry with a regatta of boats rowed by men, young boys and even women. The procession down the Grand Canal was in honour of the Duke and Duchess, who sat regally in upholstered chairs on the balcony of the loggia nodding and waving in approval.

But the third Sunday of September was the one that Emilia awaited. It was at this time that Burano celebrated the Fish Festival. Emilia recalled that her aunts and mother would always be on that charming island to help prepare the huge cauldrons of polenta to accompany the plates of fish and jugs of fresh white wine. Emilia had not dreamed that after her marriage she would be on Burano to help with this, her favourite, celebration.

And so it was that she joined her mother on the long boat ride to Burano on the Monday before the Festival. It would take the whole week to grind and sift and clean the cornmeal imported from the Veneto for the polenta. Rich sweet Gorgonzola cheese, ivory coins of oil preserved goat cheese, and thick cream with honey were the types of toppings used by the locals to flavour the sun-yellow ribbons of smooth polenta ladled onto shallow wooden plates.

Her uncles were working alongside the other men to lay nets in the richest fishing areas and to harvest the mussels and clams from the shallows.

Emilia was sitting on a low stool over a large canvas sail upon which baskets of the dry cornmeal had been poured. She formed part of the circle of women picking any stones or clods of soil from the meal. It was soothing work and inspired conversations on many subjects, but generally the topics were the kitchen or family or the mysteries of the bedroom.

"So, Emilia, how is your life in Venice? We thought we would never see you again after the theatre of Venice lured you away?" asked one of the older Buranese women who had known her mother and aunts since they had been young girls themselves.

"Yes, Auntie Rosa, Venice is magnificent, it is true. But for all the pomp and pageantry, the islands will always be my home and the waters of the lagoon in my veins," Emilia was pleased to make this proclamation. She would always be the daughter of Chioggia, first and resident of Venice second.

"But, come on, Rosa, ask what is really on our minds," her Aunt Mariella urged with a bawdy chuckle.

"Mariella, you are incorrigeable. Let the poor girl have her secrets." Faustina scolded her sister, but was smiling at the same time.

"Aunt Mariella, I am sure it is as it is in your own household: Francesco is the head and I am the neck, no?" The women threw their back heads and flashed their eyes at Mariella, cheering Emilia's answer.

Then Emilia was more serious. "Francesco is a wonderful and caring husband. He is handsome, gentle and," she paused for effect, "in *all* the rooms of the house pleases me."

Again, the women approved. It was clear to them that Emilia was happy and settled into her new role. Faustina beamed with pride at her daughter's ability to hold her own in this circle of women.

On Sunday Emilia stood in front of a huge metal cauldron with her legs spread for ballast and her hands wrapped around the stem of the long wooden paddle sunk into the still watery gold liquid of the polenta. The cauldron was set firmly on a metal ring over a wood fire, which was tended by a young island boy, proud to play his part in preparing the festival.

There Emilia would stand for over an hour carefully and continuously stirring with the large flat paddle. As the polenta thickened it would become harder and harder to stir steadily and Emilia knew that she would be drenched with perspiration by the time the polenta was ready to be dished up to the revellers. The polenta must never be allowed to rest long enough to stick to the bottom of the cauldron.

One of the women would stop by occasionally to sample the liquid, add a dollop of sweet butter or a small pinch of coarse sea salt. This was a ritual observed down centuries and was taken as seriously as any religious ritual. It was considered a *bruta figura*, an embarrassment, if your cauldron of polenta displayed any lumps.

The fisherman began to stoke long olive wood charcoal fires in a special brick lined trench. At the right moment, black metal grills would be positioned over the embers and then the fish would be set to cook. Again, this required careful and expert attention.

A short distance off, large vats of olive oil were heated to fry the small fishes and shrimps that had been lightly dusted with flour.

And of course, smaller cauldrons of water bubbled to receive the mussels and clams that would be quickly boiled and scooped into basket to be eaten with the fingers. The broth of the cauldron contained a head of garlic, laurel, several dried red peppers, slices of lemon and a generous pitcher of white wine. This would be conserved to become a base for rich fish soup.

"Ciao, Emilia," a deep voice greeted her and she looked up briefly from the concentration she was giving to her cauldron, expecting to see a cousin or other young man of the island.

She almost let go of the paddle, which would have spun for a moment or two on its own with the momentum of the thickening mash.

"Dario. Dario," she had lost her voice, but soon regained her composure. "How are you? I thought I might run into you in our new 'village,' but I had not expected to see you here."

He laughed. "Yes, Venice is a village. However, I have been in my workshop day in and day out. In fact, the quiet of August in the city has served me well. Emilia, I have been given an amazing commission and I have so many ideas, I can barely tear myself away from my tools."

"I see how excited your are. Tell me." Emilia was back into the cadence of her stirring and found she was able to talk easily to Dario. She felt relieved. His friendship meant a great deal to her.

"It seems that a grand new library is being built at the monastery of San Giorgio Maggiore and the design calls for alcoves to hold a series of carved statues of the saints. Longhena, the architect, has seen my work and asked specifically for me to carve a number of the figures. It is a great honour."

"Oh, Dario, it sounds like a wonderful project. Your work must be magnificent." Emilia was sincerely pleased to see her friend's talent recognized. "What is required by the commission? Are you under a strict deadline to complete the figures?"

"Fortunately I have almost six years to complete the figures. I have estimated about one statue per year. Some are more complicated than others and, of course, the grain of the wood will play a role in how I create the drape and the stance of the figures. Four of the figures are men and two women. It is a challenge, but I know I am up to it. My maestro has also supported Longhena's choice."

"How did you manage to come to the festival?" Emilia was beginning to feel the resistance of the thickening polenta and was struggling to continue conversation with the effort of the stirring.

"I knew that my mother would welcome the chance to see me and I look forward to this festival every year, as you know. Besides, Burano is so close to Venice that I can return in the evening if I wish."

Dario noticed the beads of moisture forming on Emilia's forehead beneath the fabric of her scarf. He reached out with his handkerchief to wipe her head.

"Can I take over the stirring to give you a rest?" His hand lingered beneath the handkerchief on her cheek.

"Oh, no. Thank you, Dario. This is a woman's job and I want to show that I am able."

He put the handkerchief in his vest pocket. "Well, I will leave you to it, then. Emilia, how are you? I have been so busy telling my news, I have rudely failed to hear yours!

"I am fine, Dario. Dear Dario, I am so pleased to have your friendship. It has been wonderful seeing you again. Take care."

As he moved off into the crowd, Emilia thought of how her life could have been very different, if she and Dario..."But, no. I must not even consider what could have been," she thought. "I have my life. It is done." She stirred more vigorously and watched the vortex forming in the centre of her cauldron.

Back in Chioggia news had arrived about the battles near Crete. While the Venetian fleet was cruising off Crete, a corsair fleet from Barbary entered the Adriatic. The Venetians attacked the Turks, bombarded the forts and captured their galleys. The Sultan arrested Alvise Contarini, a Venetian official on Crete. However, through diplomacy, an all out war was averted. Tension with the Turks was always present, but the immediate crisis had been resolved.

In the course of the battle, the Venetians had lost one ship and several others had been damaged. Don Lorenzo held a special mass for the sailors and said special prayers for Emilia's Ensign. And so October passed with no hard news of the name of the galley that had gone down, nor names of any sailors who were injured or killed.

Emilia felt ill with worry. This was a part of her marriage bargain that she had not considered before now. This was why her father had wanted her to be in Chioggia during Francesco's forays. If she had been so worried and sick in Venice, she would have been alone. Here, on the island, she had her mother, Don Lorenzo and a community of friends who would be there to support her through the worst, if necessary.

It was in the second week of November that a long boat rowed by Venetian sailors arrived at the harbour in Chioggia. A weathered young Ensign disembarked. His arm was held close to his body with a wide bandage and the arm of his tunic was empty and tucked into his belt. Word travelled to the Baseggio household that Ensign Francesco Gradenigo had landed and requested his wife to meet him.

Emilia was up to her elbows in kneading flour for pasta. She had flour on her nose, in her hair, and on her apron. At the news, she quickly tore off her apron and ran to the harbour. She was unsure of how a wife should behave in this instance, so she slowed her run to a fast walk and tried to pat her hair into some semblance of order, thus, transferring still more flour to her dark curls.

As soon as she saw Francesco her eyes filled with tears. He was hurt and looked thin and tired. She ran to him and threw her arms around his waist.

" My love. My love," she sobbed.

"Oh. Oh," he cried. "You are covering my tunic with flour. Don't cry, Dearest. I am fine. I am fine." He lifted her with his one free arm and hugged her to him so firmly that she felt the breath squeezed from her.

When Emilia looked up, she saw he was smiling, but also grimacing. He had been hurt.

"What are your injuries? We must take care of you."

"I leapt from the yard arm and landed badly; luckily I held my sword in my other hand and was able to smite the cur who was preparing to kill my general!" He smiled broadly. "I have broken a small bone, apparently. A collarbone. It will heal quickly, but I must keep my arm immobile."

Emilia felt relief and pride. He had saved the life of his general. He was a hero.

The worry that had plagued Emilia had dissipated, but the feeling of illness seemed to increase. Soon she understood that it was the common illness of a woman expecting a child and she embraced the discomfort. She was to be a mother. The mother of her beloved's son!

Francesco's collarbone mended quickly, as he had predicted and when he seemed to be completely fit and rested Emilia decided she would give him their exciting news. Her mother was sworn to secrecy, because Emilia knew that this news would be shouted from the belltower in her small village.

Together she and her mother prepared a special autumn feast for Francesco. Emilia made delicate dough and twisted it expertly into small hat shapes filled with sweet pumpkin, seasoned with nutmeg and cinnamon. The sauce was a simple fresh butter with sage. This was a dish that even Emilia could enjoy in her delicate state. Certain smells could put her off, but the smell of cinnamon was almost soothing.

Next they poached the sweet sole fish in mild herbs to be served on a bed of fresh spinach that would soften and cook from the heat of the fish. Finally, Emilia made a torte of citron that was dusted with finely ground sugar.

After the meal, Francesco sipped a sweet wine. He leaned back in his chair, satisfied and content. The colour in his face had evened out and his cheeks had regained their smoothness with rest and good food. The atmosphere of the island had a healing effect.

"I have to go back to Venice soon, my dear. Will you stay here on the island or do you feel like coming back with me?" Francesco had closed his eyes and seemed to be completely relaxed. "It is as you wish, Emilia. I know how happy you are here and I will be preparing to sail again in a week."

"I have thought about it, Francesco. It is true that these months have been wonderful for me. I have the benefit of two houses now. I am very lucky." She was choosing her words carefully, because she knew this was an important announcement. "I would like to join you in Venice, even if it is only for a week. You see, we have reason to celebrate and with you leaving soon, I want to spend every moment together discussing the future of our child."

The chair came forward with a bang and Francesco's eyes sprang open. "Our child! Emilia, do you mean... we are to have a child?" He stood up so quickly the chair fell backward and he drew her to him. "You are so wonderful and clever, my darling."

Emilia laughed and hugged him in return. "Clever? But it was easy, no?"

The next morning her mother was released from her vow of silence and to the calls from many well-wishers, the couple boarded the boat to journey home to Venice.

Chapter Fourteen

————————————

*B*ack in Venice Emilia established a daily routine. She would go off to the shops with Carolina, or even on her own, now that she knew which stalls to favour. The two sisters would keep the apartment clean and help Emilia prepare dough for pasta and wash the lettuces. Some days, they would allow her to insist that they stay to have lunch with her. Then she would release them for the rest of the day and prepare a light supper for herself.

Emilia had persuaded Francesco to allow her to remain in the city when his ship sailed. In her present state she felt it better not to travel too much and she welcomed the peace and quiet of her empty apartment. He relented and agreed that she would be cared for well with Carolina and Angelina on hand. He planned to alert his mother in Asiago that on her occasional trips to Venice, she ought to stop in and visit Emilia. And, of course, Stefano and Giustiana were nearby if Emilia needed them for company.

Emilia especially enjoyed exploring Venice on her own; getting lost in mysterious streets, so narrow she could almost touch both sides with her shoulders. She would skip over footbridges that sometimes ended in a private garden or at the heavy handled door of a private home, and then backtrack to the paths that open up and border the canals. Soon the café owners would greet her by name and she began to feel that Venice was indeed becoming her city.

Late in November on her errand to the market, Emilia decided to explore the Dogana da Mar which bordered the city on the Canale della Giudecca. Emila knew of the fabulous cathedral being built there to fulfil a vow made to the Blessed Virgin to mark the end to the plague. It had been ten years since the epidemic had subsided. She had been a young child, but people still talked in hushed tones of the scourge. The cathedral was near completion. Emilia remembered seeing the various stages of construction from the ferries that carried her from Chioggia to Venice through the canal. She recalled how white and majestic it looked with an enormous dome, a pair of belltowers and a smaller dome, that had just been placed.

Before she was too laden down with produce or fish, Emilia hailed a gondola to traverse the Grand Canal and take her to the landing platform for the Dogana. Shaped like a ship's hull, this was the customs house for goods arriving to Venice by sea. A golden statue of Fortune overlooking a giant globe topped the building, symbolizing that the fortune of Venice held sway over the world.

Emilia walked from the landing toward the massive structure of the cathedral. Off to the side, men were shaping marble into statuary, tapping with wooden mallets against small chisels to create decorations for final placement on the structure. Apprentices were gently smoothing with files or special emery clothes to polish the pieces.

The interior of the basilica was complete and Emilia walked through the heavy bronze doors into the cold white air of the church. The first thing she noticed was the height of the central dome. It seemed to rise into the heavens; it looked airy and light despite its bulk. Six small chapels spread beneath the dome, each dedicated to a particular saint.

Emilia looked down and was mesmerized by the intricate rose design of the coloured marbles on the floor. The pattern of roses symbolized the rosary and an inscription stated that the health and salvation of Venice was due to the protection of the Virgin.

As she was staring at the Latin inscription someone had taken her elbow.

"May I carry your packages for you, Signora?" The grip tightened and turned her slightly.

"Dario! What ever are you doing here?" Emilia was too surprised to react.

"My patron, Baldassare Longhena has built this basilica and I often come here to see the progress of the project and to watch the stone cutters. It is quite a different technique than we wood carvers use, but I find it even more amazing the way these artisans can instil such tender emotion into the faces of the cold marble figures." He looked around the interior of the cathedral and then back at Emilia. "It is a wonder, no?"

"Breathtaking," she said. "Is your workshop nearby?"

"Not at all. But the boat ride clears my head and helps me when I return. In fact, I am headed back there now. It is near the boatyards. Come with me. I am so anxious to show you what I am doing."

"Do you think it would be all right? I know how sensitive the builders in Chioggia are when it comes to women and boats."

"The carvers are not so sensitive. Do come. I won't keep you so long that your fruits will over ripen!" he joked, taking her packages and leading her back to the entrance of the basilica.

The brisk November wind whipped at the edges of her scarf as the water taxi brought them to the walls of *Arsenale*. The boatyards were connected to the Basin of San Marco by a narrow canal. The carpenters worked in *Arsenale Nuova* and *Arsenale Nouvissimo* where they were trained as joiners and shipwrights.

Dario and Emilia disembarked at a small landing on the Galeazzi Canal and she followed him to an elegant looking stone structure. Heavy blocks of volcanic stone rose several stories. When they passed through the tall wooden doors, tall enough to allow a galley to pass, Emilia was struck by the rich smell of the wood. The ceiling of the interior was at least ten meters high and stone walls were latticed with small balconies forming studio spaces for the artisans. Not all the carvers were working on standing figures. Most were creating panels with bas-relief, or carving decorative shapes for churches and ships.

Dario's workshop was spacious; light from large windows flooded into the area, illuminating the burnished wood of some finished carvings. Pinned along a beam were numerous sketches and detailed drawings of figures. Executed by Longhena, himself, these "cartoons" were meant as a guide for Dario's creations.

"I have been studying figure drawing and learning the musculature of the face, hands, and feet in particular. The carving of drapery has come almost naturally to me." He was running his hands over a tall rectangular block of wood. It was walnut with a subtle grain and burl.

"These are beautiful," said Emilia looking at the many drawings. The faces were all distinct and evocative. She noticed the neat row of tools: chisels, wooden mallets and drills, which looked like tiny bows to hold the drill bits or miniature "arrows".

On the floor were neatly swept piles of chips and scattered splinters of the wood. She knelt to touch one curl of walnut.

"Take it," he urged, "as a souvenir of your visit," he bent down beside her and handed her the delicate wood chip. "Here. Would you like to sit while I do a little work?" Dario offered her a low stool.

"No, no, thank you. Dario, I fear I must get back to the apartment. The sisters will wonder why I have taken so long." She took his hand in hers. "I feel so fortunate to know such a great talent, Dario. Your work will live on long past our lifetimes. The statues in the library will inspire deep study and thought. And those carvings you create for churches in Venice and beyond will be eternal tokens to God. You are using your skills to make our world more beautiful and gentle."

He was very touched by this outpouring from his dearest friend. His eyes held hers and must have transmitted that he still did and always would love her. However, he held her in deep respect and would never jeopardize her station as wife and soon to be mother. Moreover, he knew that her husband was placed in constant danger in his profession and Dario hoped she would always feel she could lean on him if she needed to as a friend.

"Emilia, I have heard of the exciting news and congratulate you and Francesco. I know you will make a wonderful mother to your child." He raised her hand to his lips. "I would be so honoured if you would feel that you could come and be my muse. Could you consider it?"

"Perhaps I could come on occasion, Dario. Now that I know where your workshop is located, I could pass by and sit for a time. I am fascinated by the idea of creating delicate drapery and faces from blocks of wood. Thank you." She released her hand from his. "Now I really must go. Will you help me to the boat?"

"Of course, my dear. This way," he led her down the small staircase to the stones of the building floor and they exited the building. He greeted a colleague who was disembarking and helped Emilia into the craft.

"Do you need me to accompany you?" he asked solicitously.

"No, no, Dario," she demurred, "You must get back to work!" She smiled and waved as the boat pulled from the landing.

When she got home, the sisters were waiting at the door of the building for her, looking anxious.

"What is it, Carolina? Is it word from Signor Francesco?" Emilia's heart contracted as if in a vice of fear and she felt her baby shift inside her.

"No, Signora. Everything is fine as far as we know. It is just that…that…" Angelina broke in, "Signora Gradenigo is upstairs. She has been waiting for you."

The three hurried up to the apartment, Emilia having handed the packages to the girls and taken off her scarf.

"Forgive me, Signora. I am sorry," Emilia curtseyed quickly and moved into the salon. "I have kept you waiting."

"Not to worry, my dear," Signora Gradenigo did not look at all inconvenienced and reseated herself in the chair wherein she had been reclining. "I am only in Venice for the day and I promised Francesco I would stop in to see if you needed anything." Her eyes were focused on Emilia's hem. "Have you been to the markets?"

"Yes, I had gone to the *mercato* and then on a whim decided to visit the new basilica, Santa Maria della Salute. It is nearing completion and I had only seen it from the boat coming from Chioggia. It is magnificent." Emilia's own eyes travelled to the point of interest, her hem, and she saw that there seemed to be a fringe of wood chips and curls adorning it. She felt her face burn.

"It *is* stupendous!" Signora Gradenigo exclaimed. Carolina brought a tray with mulled wine in goblets and olives in a dish; she set it on a low table next to Signora Gradenigo's chair. "Thank you, my dear." The girl bowed slightly and left the room. "Let me help you, Emilia." The woman brought the goblet to Emilia and looked closely at her. "Are you feeling well? You are not overdoing it, are you?"

"No, no. I am feeling very well. Now that I am past the early months I have a good appetite and am gaining kilos gradually. At this point I can even feel the child moving occasionally. Truly it is miraculous. I feel very blessed." She took the wine and with her other hand stroked her slightly rounded belly.

"You and Francesco will have a beautiful child; of that I am certain," she smiled warmly at Emilia.

Signora Gradenigo stayed for lunch and they talked lightly about a variety of topics before Francesco's mother took her leave to journey back to *terrafirma,* as the mainland was called. Emilia felt tired and welcomed her chance to rest at the end of the impromptu visit.

The sisters had cleared the kitchen and left for the day. On the sideboard were fruit and a plate of cold vegetables in oil and a basket of fresh bread for dinner. Emilia rarely called them back for dinner and this light supper was easier for her to digest.

Emilia's dreams that afternoon were filled with a kaleidoscope of conflicting images. There was Francesco leaning over her, his eyes burning into hers. Was it passion or something else? Before she could identify the emotion, another image came. This time it was the Salute and at the top of the dome was the statue of the Virgin. It was carved, not in gilded bronze, but in wood. No, she was not at the basilica; she was in the workshop with Dario. He touched her face, as if to outline the features. He looked so sad. She asked him not to forsake her.

She awoke with a start. The room was dark and she was still in her slip. She had slept past the dinner hour and the moon was setting. She felt her heart pounding in her chest. What did it mean?

She went to the kitchen and drank a cool glass of water. It calmed her and the stone floor felt cool beneath her feet. The air in the apartment was brisk as the fires had been banked for the night and would not be rebuilt until morning when the sisters came. But she felt refreshed rather than chilled by the low temperature.

Emilia walked into the salon and looked out the windows across the Venetian skyline. Could she see a dim outline of the Salute? She closed her eyes and prayed,

"Blessed Virgin, bring me a healthy child."

Chapter Fifteen

*F*rancesco was home for the month of December. Despite being infidels, the Turks chose not to make trouble in the holy month of Christ's birth. The couple had been invited along with her parents to spend several days leading up to Christmas at Ca' Foscari with Stefano and Maria Giustiana's parents. They were especially anxious to see Vittorio's reaction to the *Befana*, the crone who left gifts for good children on the Epiphany.

The palace was beautifully adorned with garlands of greenery, vases of rare flowers and swags of silken fabrics, the commodity of the Foscari family. The rooms were incensed with the smell of the evergreens and flowers. Gay fires burned in all the hearths and the family balanced festive meals with quiet conversations in the salon and traditional card games of the season.

Vittorio was adorable and seemed to relish all the attention from his grandmothers and grandfathers. He begged to be lifted onto Emilia's lap and seemed to calm at the warmth of the baby inside her as he sucked his thumb and stroked her belly contentedly, much to everyone's amusement. His hair had turned a very pale blond and his almond eyes had begun to mirror the beauty of Giustiana. Emilia loved to bury her nose in the fine silk of his hair and smell his baby skin. Every fibre of her being was feeling maternal and content.

The family was gathered at the table relishing servings of the traditional *zampone*, pig's foot-shaped sausage, and lentils, each grain symbolic of coins. The meal was the traditional New Year's dinner, representing wealth and prosperity in the New Year; in fact, it was the beginning of a new decade – 1640. Signor Foscari raised a glass of fine sparkling wine and toasted the family.

"To the family! May we thrive and increase," he looked pointedly to his daughter. "We will need many sons to carry on our family honour in business."

"Here, here," Baseggio chimed, beaming with pride at Emilia and Francesco.

Francesco asked permission to stand and make a toast. First he thanked the Foscari family for their hospitality and then he raised his glass to Emilia.

"To my beautiful wife who carries the next heir. She is my safe harbour and my firm anchor."

A great cheer went up around the table and Francesco drank deeply. As he sat down he noticed tears in the corners of Emilia's eyes and squeezed her hand under the table.

In February Francesco was off to sea once more and Emilia lapsed back into her routine in Venice. She was tiring more easily now as the baby grew rapidly and often kept her awake at night with somersaults and kicking. "Surely this one is a fighter," she thought.

Early in the month she felt restless and took her lacework in a small cloth drawstring bag and boarded a gondola for Arsenale. She had not spoken to or seen Dario since November and was curious to view the progress of his carving. She stayed tucked into rugs under the canopy as the boat rounded the Dogana and headed to the open Bacino di San Marco and Riva degli Schiavoni, the shipyards.

She stepped through the tall wooden doors and called up to the loft. *"Permesso*? -May I come in?"

"Of course!" Dario practically leapt down the short staircase to greet her. "I was beginning to give up hope that my muse would come and I am in a quandary at the moment with my carving. This is providential!" He kissed her cheeks and took her hooded cape and hung it on a brass hook at the base of his loft.

When she saw the half completed carving, she gasped. It was so lifelike. The clothes were draped so delicately that it seemed a breeze from the doors would shift them. The hands were detailed down to the tracery of veins and valleys between the bone and muscle. In the right hand was a shallow circle. Then she realized; it was the beginnings of a carved wheel. St. Catherine! The walnut was still grooved in places by the chisel marks, but here and there the wood shone as if it had been oiled. The shape of the head was solid, but had not been outlined with features as yet.

"What do you think so far?" Dario was like a small boy looking for approval for his sandcastle.

"I cannot speak, Dario. It is…it is amazing. It is truly beautiful." She approached the figure that stood taller than Dario. "May I touch her?"

"Of course. The wood is organic. It is alive. You will feel the warmth and pulse of it," he took her hand in his and ran her palm across the folds of the skirt down to the feet.

"It is majestic, Dario. It is so elegant. You are a master." She felt the details of the hem of the skirt. The pattern he had carved was of an intricate lace. Much like the pattern from his home island.

"Sit! Sit!" He pulled a sturdy chair with a back from the corner of the loft. It had a cushion and a lap robe was draped over the arm. "I have prepared for you. This is your place."

"I can only stay an hour, Dario, but I am so glad I made the journey. I have been thinking about your work and wondering how it was progressing." She settled into the chair and put the cushion behind her lower back for support. "I had intended to work on my lace while I watched you, but I am sure I will be unable to concentrate."

"St. Catherine of Alexandria is an important figure. Only two women are included in the grouping for the library at San Giorgio: St. Ceclia, the patron saint of musicians, and Catherine. She carries the wheel that was meant to be her death in martyrdom. As they bound her to it, an angel sent by God broke the wheel in two. She was still put to death, however, for teaching the doctrines of the church to the learned men of Alexandria." He began to gather tools and set them on a high stool near him. He laid them on a small square of chamois cloth that was softened and oiled.

Dario spent the hour putting more details onto the hair and drape of shawl of the figure. It seemed he would barely caress or outline a place on the wood and the shape or curve would alter and come to life. Emilia could not take her eyes off of his hands.

At the end of the hour, she insisted he stay in the loft and she would walk through the biting wind to the landing where gondoliers were always waiting, as traffic to and away from the Arsenale was steady. Venice needed many ships to maintain its reputation as ruler of the Adriatic, Mediterranean and beyond.

Emilia could not stay away from the workshop. She was drawn there and soon was able to focus somewhat on her lacework. She would trim the baby's linens with the handiwork of the generations of Buranese women and Dario would perform the magic of his handiwork on the wood. Soon a faint hint of features began to emerge on St. Catherine.

One day when Emilia arrived, the figure was pushed into a corner and covered with a long canvas cloth. A new block of almost untouched wood stood in the centre of the loft. The tall stool held coarser chisels and larger mallets.

"I am beginning a new piece. I have set St. Catherine aside for a time. I need to ponder how to proceed with her.' Dario answered the questioning look on Emilia's face. "This will be one of the Evangelists – St. Matthew." He stroked the wood tenderly and began to smooth the corner edges with a lathe. "I have been studying a series of paintings by an artist from Rome and the humanistic facial expressions and the realistic musculature intrigues me. His name is Messina, but he is called 'Caravaggio.'" As he spoke long curls of wood seemed to bloom from the blade of the lathe and the petals floated to the floor. He paused and stepped back to see the work from a distance. Before returning to the block, he stooped and picked up a long curl, which he placed whimsically in the coils of Emilia's hair.

"You look very beautiful today, Emilia. Your face has a translucency that is unusual and your eyes are deeper and more liquid than I recall." He held her chin between in thumb and forefinger, studying her features closely. She squirmed slightly under his scrutiny.

"Do not fear, my sweet, I am looking as an artist, not as the man who would have taken you in the bottom of a boat if given the chance." He released her chin and turned once again to his carving. "You look like a Chioggian Madonna, so beautiful."

At the end of the hour, Emilia gathered her lace and linen and Dario helped her on with her cape.

"Take care, Emilia. I think of you every day and it is such a joy to have you for my muse," he raised her hand to his lips before it disappeared into her fur muff and she disappeared out the doors.

On the landing there was a good deal of activity. Sailors, shipwrights and workers were jostling for a place on the platform at the approach of a large gondola. Emilia recognized the crest of Francesco's boat on their tunics and greeted the men. Touching their hands to their tri-cornered hats, they stepped aside, making room for her on the boat before crowding on themselves. The shipwrights called colloquial farewells and waved over their shoulders as they headed back to their labours. Emilia huddled into her cape and watched the *Arsenale* disappear into the mist.

It was the last time she would travel there.

Chapter Sixteen

L ove, honour and obey. She had vowed.

As Stefano and Don Lorenzo stood on either side of her, helping her walk down the narrow corridor of the prison which led toward the wider staircases to the Supreme Tribunal, she pondered how far those vows would extend – beyond death? But, no, it was *until* death. But if something preceded death? Was there a release from the vows when the husband broke the laws of the Republic? When he instigated a murder? To whom was she expected to be loyal...ultimately?

"Signora, be strong. The Inquisitors are only trying to ascertain if you were a part of the intrigue. They are looking for information to exonerate you, I am convinced of this. You need only relate what occurred that night in Cyprus. I know it has been a shock to you and your wound was nearly fatal, but now you are healed and this unpleasantness can be at an end." Santacroce was walking more quickly and had to alter his pace to drop back and speak to Emilia.

She was only able to look straight ahead and put one foot before another. She stumbled slightly on the smooth marble stairs. The rich tapestries on the walls depicted pastoral scenes that seemed idyllic and carefree. She wished she could step into the fabric and join the nobles, goddesses and satyrs in their rollick. Further along, stern portraits of Doges, Cardinals and Senators seemed to look accusatorily at her; their eyes were burning into her heart to seek out her guilt. She felt dizzy and yet every fibre and nerve of her being seemed alert, magnifying all the sensations: the grip on her upper arms by Stefano and Don Lorenzo, the echoes of their steps in the marble hallway, the scent of the sea which permeated the air even through the thick walls of the palace. The cleansing sea. The soothing sea.

"Here we are." Santacroce stopped their halting march and motioned Stefano and the priest to chairs flanking the tall wooden doors of the chamber, the Supreme Tribunal of the Doge. The Council of Ten had established them over a century earlier and their name instilled terror even in those innocent, but under suspicion. They could be manipulated. They could judge falsely.

The door closed behind the lawyer and Emilia with a velvet thud. A guard stepped in front of it and the three Inquisitors motioned for Santacroce to approach with his client.

"Excellencies, this is Emilia Baseggio, the wife of Francesco Gradenigo of Assiago, the Ensign known as Iago. She is here to be questioned about the tragic events that took place almost four months ago in Cyprus. Her husband attempted to silence her with his dagger, but, luckily, she survived his attack and is here to shed light on the crimes." He was warming to his subject.

"As you can see, she is a young woman without guile, a mother. Excellencies, this woman has behaved as a loyal subject of the Republic, even at the risk of her own life. Rather than being accused of treason, she should be decorated for her bravery in exposing the plot against the state..." he was prepared to continue with his opening remarks when *il rosso*, the scarlet robed inquisitor, raised his hand.

"Thank you, Dottore Santacroce, but we are here to decide the veracity of this woman's testimony and to determine her guilt, or, as you claim, her heroism," his voice dripped sarcasm on the final word. Clearly he was not to be swayed by the lawyer's arguments. He wanted to hear the facts.

"Speak, Signora. Tell all you remember and all you know about the deaths of Desdemona, General Othello, Roderigo, and the wounding of our Governor Cassio," the black robed interrogator spoke. He looked like a demon from a fresco of the Last Judgement in his dark robe and tall pointed hat. His eyes pierced into hers and she was forced to lower her own or lose whatever nerve she could muster.

She cleared her throat. It seemed months since she had spoken and she would have asked for a glass of water, if she were not so stricken with fear. And yet a calm seemed to descend. What did it matter at this point? She seemed not to care for her own life. There seemed nothing holding her to this earth. Even her young daughter would be better off without her. She stood taller and began her testimony.

"Excellencies, I only understood the extent of the intrigue after Desdemona had been smothered by her husband. He was wild with jealous rage and was convinced that she had cuckolded him with his

Lieutenant. It was a complete fabrication. Desdemona loved the Moor and would have given him her life if he had asked for it. In fact, she claimed that he did *not* murder her in her dying breath. She was martyred for a lie. That lie was engineered by my husband, the Ensign Iago."

The Inquisitors leaned forward as a body, focusing closely on every word of her statement. She paused only for breath before continuing.

"I was not privy to the details of my husband's plot. I believe the motivation for his revenge was pride and betrayal. Francesco felt that Cassio's promotion was an insult to his own years of service. Francesco had dedicated his life to the service of the Republic and had saved the General's life several times in the heat of battle. Francesco followed his captain into the fray and risked death. Francesco admired, no, he loved, his General, " Emilia swayed on her feet. "Loved him, perhaps, too much," her voice dropped to almost a whisper.

As Emilia spoke the full understanding of the emotions behind Francesco's acts became clear to her. He *had* loved Othello. And, like a spurned lover, Othello's favouritism toward Cassio enraged Ensign Iago.

Clearly his revenge turned on how to hurt the man for betraying him. Francesco knew that Desdemona was the weak point. Othello loved her to distraction and felt himself unworthy of her returned love. Francesco had identified the bond: she was the General's general. She could be used to twist him on the rack of his own jealousy and insecurity. That was the key.

"Othello raged at Desdemona on the word from my husband that she had betrayed him. I did not understand the General's erratic and cruel behaviour at the time. But Othello smothered the pure Desdemona on the word of the Ensign."

"Very well, Signora. Can you elaborate on the testimony of Lodovico concerning a token given by Othello to his wife and found in Cassio's possession?" *il rosso* asked the pointed question which brought burning blood of shame into Emilia's cheeks. Her reaction did not go unnoticed by the Inquisitors. Was this the proof they were seeking as to her guilt?

"The token, as you call it, was an embroidered handkerchief given to Desdemona as a wedding gift by the General. He claimed it was a gift to his own mother by a magus from Africa, his home. He told Desdemona it was charmed. My husband petitioned me to bring it to him if I had a chance. The girl dropped it in her chamber in a distracted moment and I delivered it to the Ensign. I had no idea of his intention, but I should have known it would lead to some bad end." She lowered her head and spoke more to herself that to the Tribunal, "if only I had known. I should have guessed."

"Signora, if you please, what exactly was the purpose of your presence in Cyprus? Were the ships not commissioned to go to battle with a Turkish fleet? It hardly seems appropriate that women were allowed to travel with the navy into war," the black robed man seemed incensed at the thought of this distraction to the duties of the sailors. He harrumphed loudly to emphasize his disdain for the idea of women interfering in the man's realm.

"My husband entreated me to join the party," she had no sooner spoken than the three questioners seemed to nod and straighten. Now they were getting somewhere. The plot had taken shape prior to the sailing and the arrival in Cyprus. Clearly the intrigue was laced with a far-reaching strategy and not merely an act of passionate revenge on Othello. It was premeditated.

"Desdemona had eloped with the General and been disowned by her father." Simmering outrage met this proclamation and Emilia went on her guard. "Brabantio was heartbroken, it seems, by his daughter's headstrong disobedience and in the moment spoke harshly. The Senate were concerned with the urgency of the situation in Cyprus and hastily accepted Othello's plea to have his wife join him. Francesco explained this to me and asked if I would be willing to go along with the young girl as her helpmate. It seemed a request that I could not refuse, knowing that Francesco would do anything for his General and the well-being of the General's wife."

She looked hard into their eyes. "I made a vow before God to honour and obey my husband. I wanted to help in his suit to be reinstated and promoted, as was his due." She took a chance. "He was wronged. It does not excuse his actions, but he was wronged, Excellencies. He fought valiantly for Venice. He was not a traitor to the Republic." She broke down at this point and Santacroce took her arm as sobs prevented her from speaking further.

"Take her away, Dottore. There is nothing more we can achieve with this interview." *il rosso* disgustedly waved his hand at the lawyer and the accused. Santacroce backed out of the chamber pulling Emilia gently before him.

Back in her cell, Emilia continued to sob. She collapsed into a chair. She was exhausted by the ordeal of the interrogation and was trying to reconstruct what she had said to ascertain if she had told all she needed to or if she had somehow misspoken.

Stefano stroked her head. "You did well, Emilia. Dottore Santacroce claims you spoke very well and shed light on the tragedy. Don't cry, my sparrow, you did well."

His words soothed her somewhat and although her body was wracked by shudders, she stopped crying. "Mamma sent you some food. We will have a celebratory lunch right here with you, dear one."

Don Lorenzo was directing the guard to bring a table through the narrow door and to gather more chairs.

"I must leave you, now, Signor. Signora. I will check with you in several days. The Tribunal will digest what they have heard and compare it to other testimony. Nothing will be decided for a number of days. Every effort is being made to impress them on your innocence, my dear. Do not despair." The lawyer shook hands with Stefano and bowed slightly to Lorenzo as he left.

Stefano unpacked several baskets with plates, glasses, bread and pasta wrapped carefully in linen. It was the pumpkin tortellini she had prepared for Francesco when she told him he was to become a father; the smell of the cinnamon only made Emilia begin to weep again. She felt so homesick for Chioggia and wished she could lay down on the bottom of a boat under a canvas and be spirited home.

"Mamma," she sobbed.

Chapter Seventeen

*M*id-July brought the *zu e zo per i ponti*, or up and down the bridges, with the traditional battles and the spectacles of *guerra de canne*. This year Francesco let other sailors take part, but he was on hand to cheer. Emilia in her confinement stayed home, but heard cheers and shouts through the windows facing the canal. After the spectacle she knew that Francesco would celebrate any victories or drown sorrows of defeat with his crew at the bars along the canals. She did not expect him to be home much before dawn.

For this reason she was surprised to hear the door of the apartment open noisily and slam shut.

"Francesco, is that you? Home so soon?" she pulled the dressing gown closer to herself as she left the bedroom.

"Were you expecting someone else, my wife? Your lover perhaps? The one you have been meeting behind my back at the Arsenale?" His words were harsh and slurred with drink. His tone steeped in rage. "And so my dear and loyal wife, I learn from my men that you have been seen at the landing along Riva degli Schiavoni. The shipyards! And perchance have you been sighted on Fondamenta de Tette with the other whores exposing their breasts!" He crashed into a table in the salon and Emilia heard glass shattering as it fell to the terrazzo. He referred to the famous street of courtesans in Venice. A favourite haunt of sailors on leave.

"Francesco. Francesco, I beg you. What are you saying? What has happened, darling?" Emilia felt dread that word had travelled back to Francesco that she had gone to the dockyards to watch Dario work. She feared he had misunderstood, but deep in her heart she knew it was a sort of betrayal. A wife does not travel unescorted in Venice. The city itself is known for its women, married or not, of ill repute. Nor does she have assignations with other men, no matter how innocent. But she *was* innocent. She had done nothing to bring dishonour to herself or her husband. However, Francesco seemed in no state to listen to reason.

"What am I to think? I have been taunted and shamed by my men. They believe I have been cuckolded, and perhaps I have been. You strumpet! You whore! Explain yourself!"

The glass was purposefully thrown to the tiles this time. He vented his rage by breaking and smashing whatever lay in his path as he stormed through the apartment. He reached the hall outside the bedroom and stood legs planted apart, arms akimbo, threatening. His face was deep scarlet, his scar almost purple. The fire in his eyes was demonic and Emilia felt terrified by the violence of his accusations.

"I have done nothing to offend you, my lord," Emilia stood her ground and forced the rising bile of fear down.

"I know our country disposition well – in Venice wives let *God* see the pranks they dare not show their husbands; their best conscience is not to leave it undone, but to keep it unknown. These women. These housewives. These whores!" He roared the word and swept down on her and holding her tightly by the arms. "What are you?"

"Your wife, Francesco. Your true and loyal wife." She stared steadfastly into his smouldering eyes. Her heart seemed frozen and she could neither take nor expel breath. Time stood still.

"Whore," he bellowed. "And some base notorious knave, some scurvy fellow has cuckolded me and made you with his child." He struck her and threw her to the floor. "I'll not have it!" He towered over her as she lay trembling. "I will kill the babe rather than raise his bastard child to call my own." He took back his boot as if to kick her, but she rolled under a table, screaming for help and sobbing for him to stop.

She lay for what seemed like hours under the table on the cold tiles. She heard him stomping through the apartment and then she thought she heard him leave. A draught from the opened door blew across the floor where she huddled, chilling her. Finally she gathered herself enough to find her hooded cloak and she ventured into the night. She would go to Stefano and Giustiana. She would be safe there.

As the gondolier helped her into the boat, he commented on her being heavy with child. "Perhaps, Signora, you should not travel alone this way." His voice was tender and concerned.

"Thank you, Signor. It is nothing. I am fine," her voice trembled but she convinced him. "I am going to my brother's house. He and his wife are going to help me." She tried to settle onto the cushions below the canopy. A hot wind, the sirocco, whipped the water and tore at her hood. "I will be fine. As soon as I arrive, they will take care of me." Emilia felt she would swoon, but vowed to hold on for the short journey to safety.

The gondolier raised the alarm and Stefano's servant opened the door in his nightshirt and cap. Emilia had fainted as she tried to disembark from the boat. Her waters had broken and she needed assistance immediately. Giustiana sent a servant to fetch the midwife and Stefano carried Emilia up to the guest room. She roused for a moment and tried to speak, but her brother stroked her head and told her to rest.

"The midwife will be here soon. Perhaps your baby could not wait any longer to join us. It will be all right, my darling. Everything will be fine." He held her hand as a sudden pain swept her body and lifted her slightly. The contraction lasted less than a minute, but was strong enough to cause Emilia to cry out. It was more fear and grief that made the pain severe. She had prepared herself over the last six months for the moment of birth. She had been sure that she would weather that storm bravely and efficiently. But now it was sweeping her along too quickly.

The midwife arrived just as another wave of pain struck. She shooed everyone from the room and called for the servant to heat water and bring clean linens.

"But it is too soon. The baby is not due to be born for over a month," Emilia was beginning to panic.

"Stay calm, Signora, calm. Sometimes babies have their own clock. You will see. This one is anxious to be with us. We will make you comfortable. You must take shallow breaths and concentrate on preparing for each contraction of your womb. The baby will do the rest."

She moved her hands gently, but firmly over Emilia's stomach. She gently opened Emilia's legs and pushed part of her hand up the birth canal to feel inside.

"We have plenty of time. The child is in place, but there is much work to be done to widen the opening for the head. That is the purpose of the powerful muscle contractions. It is called labour since it is hard work. But you are young and strong. You will bring him forth smoothly." She swabbed Emilia's damp face with a cool compress.

Downstairs another drama was unfolding as Stefano and Giustiana wondered why Emilia had come to them alone in the middle of the night.

"I know that Francesco was off with his compatriots today; and, tonight was set aside for the usual carousing of this festival. But it is almost dawn and I would think he would have tried to find his wife. Surely if she is not at home, he will assume she is with us." Stefano was thinking out loud. The worry in his voice was palpable. He knew something was not right. In all the excitement and bustle little Vittorio had awakened. The nurse brought him to Giustiana. He was at the age where only his mother could soothe him. She held him on her shoulder and felt his head lolling as he struggled against sleep.

"I must take Vittorio back to the nursery, darling. Do not fret. I am sure that Francesco will come soon." She left Stefano to ruminate and the long night wore on until soon it was dawn.

Still Emilia's child was not born and still the labour continued fruitlessly. "What is wrong? Why is it taking so long?" Emilia was exhausted. The pains had increased and then subsided and almost stopped. The midwife was mixing an elixir and had decided to take measures into her own hands.

"Sometimes nature needs a helping hand. This will bring the contractions back and although they will be sharper and more frequent, they will produce results. Lift your head and sip this slowly, my dear." She propped Emilia's head with a pillow and offered her the warmed liquid. It smelled of anise and something stronger, medicinal.

Within moments Emilia felt her body stiffen and she involuntarily lifted her legs wider and up. Her whole body bent forward and she had an urge to bear down.

"Not yet. Not yet. Breathe, my dear. Do not bear down yet. I will tell you when." The midwife gently held Emilia's head and at the same time pressed firmly on the hard ball that her stomach had become. It seemed like every ounce of muscle had concentrated into that orb. The veins on her neck stood out, engorged with the strength of the contraction and the effort urging her to push and push. She puffed and tried with all of her being to hold back and follow the instructions of the midwife. But her body had taken over. Emilia had no control. It was as though she were standing next to the midwife watching the event helplessly.

It was midday when the midwife finally emerged from the room. At least five bowls of heated water had been taken in and empty ones brought out. There were piles of wet and bloody linens and the woman looked drained, but satisfied.

"Finally the little girl has deigned to show herself. It is a woman's prerogative to keep us waiting, no?" She smiled and held the tiny infant out to Giustiana, who had never seen such a small creature. The minute fingers barely gripped the edges of the tightly wrapped linen blanket. The baby's eyes were tightly screwed shut and the rosebud mouth puckered stoically.

"Santa Maria," Giustiana looked worried and amazed, "will she live?" The baby looked too small and frail to thrive, she thought.

"Signora, she is at least a month early to this world. Her birthing was difficult and the cord encircled her neck twice. It is a miracle that she is with us. For this reason, I believe that she will continue to grow and will thrive. She is small but strong and determined." The midwife adjusted the infant's blanket and one small eye fluttered, but did not open. The child seemed stiff rather than limp, which Giustiana felt might be a good sign.

"And my sister?" Stefano stepped forward. He was too afraid to hold the baby and was more concerned at this moment with Emilia.

"She has been through a very long ordeal. She must rest. The baby will need a wet nurse, but will not be strong enough to suck for very long. Feedings will have to be more frequent since they will be for a shorter time." The midwife was rolling down her sleeves and preparing to leave, gathering her things. "The Signora may need to have a doctor visit her. Although the baby was small, there was tearing. I have mended things as best as I could, but a doctor may want to order a poultice or an elixir for the pain of healing."

The midwife seemed reluctant to meet Giustiana's eyes. "The Signora may not be strong enough to bear more children, Signora Baseggio. However, I do not think she is ready to be given that sad news." She turned at the door. "Call me if you need me to return."

Stefano and Giustiana were too stunned to even say their thanks before the woman disappeared through the door and into the hot, strong light of the afternoon sun.

By the end of the second day Emilia had recovered enough to take some nourishment and to hold the infant. Still Francesco had not appeared and Emilia did not want to discuss his absence. Whenever she held the child, tears coursed down her cheeks. It was an odd reaction, thought Giustiana.

Finally, Stefano could stand it no longer. He went to the galley docked in the harbour and there he found his brother-in-law.

"Your wife and daughter need you, Francesco. Do you want to explain why you have not tried to see Emilia?" Stefano did not mince words. He came directly to the point and waited for Francesco to respond.

Francesco had been pacing on the ship and only stopped long enough to look directly into Stefano's eyes. "Did your sister tell you why I left the apartment?" His face darkened. "I have been shamed and betrayed."

Stefano had expected any reason but this and was dumbfounded.

"Yes, it is true," he continued. "Emilia has betrayed me with another man. I am not even convinced that this daughter you mention is my own blood." Francesco looked more like a petulant schoolboy who lost a wager than a cuckolded husband. His arms were crossed on his chest and he had tears in his eyes.

"Look, man. There is some mistake. My sister is devoted to you. She is chaste. She is not a woman to sneak around or to commit immoral acts. She is good and loyal. I am sure that there is some innocent explanation for whatever it is you think has happened." He reached out and put his hand on Francesco's arm. "Do you love her?"

"I loved the woman I believed had vowed to be mine and mine alone. Yes."

"That woman is Emilia. Now and forever. She has had a very difficult time of it. She needs you, Francesco. And her daughter *is* yours. I would bet my life on it." Stefano hazarded a smile, "The stubborn determination of that tiny child is certainly a trait from her stubborn father!" Francesco softened slightly. "Come home with me, brother. They need you. Please."

Although their reunion was tearful and full of pledges of love, something had happened in that night in the apartment. There was an unbridgeable gulf of mistrust on both sides and a guardedness toward each other that would shade their feelings and actions from that time forward.

Chapter Eighteen

Three years had passed since that night in July that brought Francesco and Emilia to crisis. The result had been a cooling of their passion, but all the love that they had given to each other was now focused on their small daughter, Martina. The infant had yet to say words other than a simple "mamma" and "poppi", but played contentedly and toddled after her nurse's skirts following her around the apartment in Venice. Tragedy had stricken the family the year before in the loss of Giustiana and little Vittorio to the latest outbreak of the plague in Venice. Stefano stayed to himself. Emilia could not bring herself to visit him, especially with Martina, whose presence could only bring the absence of Vittorio into a starker relief and magnify Stefano's pain.

Instead Emilia took her daughter to Chioggia frequently and stayed there with her while Francesco was at sea. Faustina adored the little girl and it was if she had regained her own daughter's childhood. Martina's vitality and charm helped offset Fautina's grief for the death of her daughter-in-law and tiny grandson. The baby's calls of "mamma" and "poppi" were soon replaced with the constant chime of "Gramma! Look, Gramma!" Faustina took the little girl everywhere with her on her errands around the island. Each summer Martina went with Faustina to Burano to be spoiled by her great aunts and uncles, and to play with her many cousins. Emilia never joined them in Burano. It puzzled Faustina, but she did not press Emilia for a reason; she respected her daughter's privacy.

Considering Francesco's doubts about his daughter, it soon became obvious that Martina was indeed a Gradenigo. It was uncanny the way she mirrored her father's looks in every way. From the shiny black curls and piercing blue eyes, to her long legs and tapered fingers, she was Francesco in miniature and she manoeuvred her way into his heart. He doted on her. She was a miracle that never ceased to amaze and entertain him. At times, Emilia felt left out, her husband and daughter were so engaged.

Oddly Emilia felt a distance from the child even from her birth. The baby was so fragile and delicate that Emilia was sure she would not survive and Emilia had protected herself by remaining unattached. When Martina passed her second birthday and finally began to crawl and walk, survival seemed less tentative. But still, Emilia knew that she had not really bonded with the baby. She feared that she would not be a good mother.

Don Lorenzo was the only one who knew the events of that night in July. Emilia confided in him the violence and circumstance of Martina's early birth. She also told him of her misgivings about mothering the little girl.

"It is not abnormal to have such feelings, my child," he reassured her. "The trauma of these events is like a wound that will take time to heal." His voice in the dim confessional was soothing to her.

"But what if I can *never* love her? I feel so guilty. I am a failure. In addition, I cannot please my husband. It is painful for me and I fear he sees it as a rejection," Emilia found herself crying. She felt exhausted from the sadness and inadequacy.

"There, there, my little angel," the priest consoled her, "Of course you love your child. It is obvious to anyone who sees you with her. You are gentle and loving. As for your concerns about your duty to your husband, these things have a way of working themselves out. The urge to share yourself in love with your husband will return in its natural course. You have given him the most precious gift of all – a legacy to his family. I know he understands and will be patient for you."

Emilia nodded her head in the dark warmth of the curtained cubicle. "Bless me father," she continued her confession and asked for his absolution and prayers.

As time passed, Emilia lost all hope of renewing her relationship with her husband. He spent more and more time aboard ship, even when it was docked in the harbour of Venice. It was as if he was avoiding her. Finally she confronted him about her fears.

"Darling, what is happening to us? It is as though we are two boats anchored in the same harbour; yet never close enough to touch. I feel so lonely. What is wrong?" She tried to gently broach the concerns she had. She stroked his arms, but he moved away from her.

"I know. I know. I have been distant. I am afraid to hurt you and also I am afraid to fail. On board the ship there are tensions as well. My General's head has been turned by a young officer, Michael Cassio. I have such a feeling of dread that I can hardly breathe." Francesco's face looked drawn and dark.

"What exactly do you fear?" Emilia felt a sudden relief that she was not the only source of his anxiety. If it was a problem at the ship, they could face it together. In a way the dilemma could bring them closer to each other.

"I know what is to come – I can feel it. Othello will give this green man, this man who has never been in battle, who has only learned from books – Othello will award him the promotion that is my due – a lieutenancy. It is outrageous. I have given all these years and even laid down my life for my General and for the Republic and this is my reward?"

Francesco sounded desperate. "I have been proven at Rhodes, at Crete and on other grounds, Christian and heathen, and this fellow, this Florentine," he spat it like a curse, "is to be given my place?" Francesco stood and began to pace the room, "I know my price, I am worth no worse a place than this appointment. Great men have approached the General in personal suit on my behalf for this promotion. But what does the Great One say: 'Oh, no, I have already decided. I have already chosen my officer, one Michael Cassio.'" Francesco was nearly apoplectic; small drops of white spittle flew from his lips as he growled the name like an epithet.

"What will you do?" Emilia was hoping to bring him back to a rational place.

"Do? What will I do?" he looked at her in shock, "Why, I will do what I have been doing for these past fifteen years! And for naught! I will serve! 'Oh, honest Iago, Oh, worthy Ancient.' Posh! I am the duteous knee-crooking slave to be cashiered when of no further use."

"No. No, Francesco. That cannot be so. You are valuable for your leadership and your loyalty. Surely the General cannot treat you so." She held his arm as he prepared to pound the fist down on the table.

"I will serve him, as I must. I follow him to serve my *turn* upon him." Dark thoughts moved like clouds across his eyes; Emilia suppressed a shudder of relief that his ire was not aimed in her direction. But his tone and expression made her heart feel dread as cold as stone.

Early one morning, less than a month after this exchange, Francesco burst into the apartment calling her name. She had not been concerned when he had stayed away all night, as this had become his habit. Often he would not venture home to her until well after the noon hour; so, this early appearance startled Emilia. Martina was in Chioggia with her grandmother and Emilia spent her time making lace or creating new recipes in the kitchen with the sisters.

"Emilia. Emilia! Are you here? Come, I must speak with you at once," he rushed into the kitchen and led her by her floured hand into their bedchamber.

"Last night Othello eloped with the daughter of a Senator, Brabantio," he was breathless. "There is hell to pay from the old man."

"But who is the woman?" Emilia was curious. Usually Giustiana had the fresh news about the scandals of the Venetian aristocracy. These tales provided some respite from Emilia's own mundane life.

"It happened late last night. Othello and the girl, Desdemona eloped. They stayed the night at the Sagittary and were called before Brabantio to explain. Meanwhile, the Ottomites are attacking Cyprus and the Council have called for the General to lead a war against the Turks." He stopped only to take a breath. He was pulling tunics and fresh linen out of his closet and bringing them into the bedroom.

"So, you must leave for Cyprus to repel the Turks?" The point about the war off the coast of Cyprus was Emilia's main concern. It sounded dangerous.

"Yes, we leave immediately. I doubt that the General has yet made the girl his full wife and her father has disowned her for the outrage of the marriage to the Moor." Francesco strode toward the closet to retrieve more fresh clothes for his journey. "You must pack some things, too. You are to join me on an escort ship to Cyprus which will carry the young wife. Once a soldier, I have been reduced to nursemaid. But never mind, it still serves me."

Emilia was trying to grasp all he had said, "Me? To follow? What is the meaning of this?" Emilia was shocked. Although she had heard of the troupes of courtesans who would arrange to arrive at an encampment to ply their trade, she had never heard of wives following men into war.

"I cannot explain it all at the moment. Hurry. You are to accompany the young wife of the General. She has been given permission by the Senate to follow her husband. Her outspoken plea seems to have touched upon their need for speed in the affair and they could not delay to debate her suit. I have been asked by Othello if you would be willing to be the helpmate of the General's new 'General'" He chuckled at his little joke, but there was a bitterness in the sound of it.

He handed her a cloth satchel and directed her to put the necessary garments into it for her journey to Cyprus. Emilia felt like a housewife whose cottage was ablaze – her decisions on what to include and what to leave behind were made in haste. But within a quarter of an hour of Francesco's announcement, they were on a gondola heading for the port to board a galley bound for Cyprus.

Chapter Nineteen

The Council of Trent in 1545 began the eight-year process of rationalizing and defining Catholic ideals within the Roman Church. Resistance to their decrees led to the Counter- Reformation and the break away of the faction that formed the Protestant Church. Prior to this time the term *family* was understood as synonymous with the corner stone of society. The configuration of the elements which constituted a legitimate family, however, was plastic.

The Council dictated that the presence of a priest was necessary for a legitimate marriage, but consensual marriages were still recognized. Stability was the key to social acceptance of such familial arrangements; thus, even into the present century of the 1600's, unblessed living arrangements were not cause for attention and were frequently acknowledged, and accepted as much as conventional marriage.

Therefore, there was little question as to the legitimacy of the bond between Brabantio's young daughter and the older General, who was a Moor. Because Othello had won such acclaim and honour in his position with the Republic, their clandestine union barely raised an eyebrow. Except for, of course, the girl's father, who was more outraged by the blow to his pride in being deceived than the fact that he had lost his daughter to the famous and decorated Moor.

Emilia learned from the girl herself that her mother died before Desdemona was two years of age. The only guardians she had known were her nurse and her father – her father being a young widower and unpractised in child rearing, and in particular with raising a daughter, kept Desdemona secluded from society as a form of protection.

The only man with whom she had had any extended contact was Othello. The General was a favourite of the Senator and often spent evenings dining in the household. He would hold the guests in thrall with his tales of the Barbary Coast, his life as an orphan captured by pirates, his escape from slavery; and, of how he eventually earned his title of General in the army of the Republic of Venice. Desdemona would shun her studies and duties to sit a short distance from where the Moor held court; his stories inspired her to dream of adventures herself. Moreover, the tragedies of his tales evoked a deep sympathy and admiration for Othello. Emilia surmised that Desdemona mistook this emotion for love.

For his part, Othello found the concern of this young girl touching. Being on his own in his life, fighting each step of the way to survive, he had never been the object of such tenderness. Desdemona's tears on his behalf reached a part of his heart that had been closed and barren. Emilia feared that Othello had mistaken his gratitude for her empathy as love for her. Thus, the bond was formed; and, to Emilia's way of thinking, the marriage was conceived where, in fact, no real love existed. Emilia sensed the union was doomed, but hoped, for the young girl's sake that real love would grow and sustain them. All this Emilia learned as she and Desdemona felt the tug of the oars moving them out of the harbour and the trade winds lift the sails of the galley that carried them away from Venice to the Mediterranean Sea and Cyprus.

Galleys, the traditional vessels of the region, were equipped with a rudder in the middle of the stern which gave them speed and mobility in manoeuvring.

The ships were moved by rowing, or, for greater speed, with sails. Being forty to sixty meters long, they varied in the numbers and arrangements of oars which ranged from one to three or four to as many as fifty to one-hundred twenty.

Lateen sails were raised on two masts, but functioned only down-wind. The galleys were outfitted with various devices of war: elevated "castles" on the prow and stern whereby lances, arrows, stones and other projectiles could be fired upon enemy boats. The "beak" which had been used in earlier times for piercing the enemy boat was replaced with a "proboscis" whereby soldiers and sailors could stream across and board the enemy boat in an attempt to occupy it. Then close battle would ensue and the boat would either repel the transgressor or be captured.

The warships in Othello's fleet were the longer type, sixty meters and equipped with sixty oarsmen and wide sails. The General would issue battle commands to the other boats by means of signal flags or with a cone hanging on the mast during the day and lamps at night. The commander or *sopracomito* was in charge of the battle on each ship and commanded the soldiers.

The warships had cast off under full sail and soon disappeared over the curve of horizon an entire day before the pair of galleys carrying Francesco and the women was ready to follow. Emilia had never been aboard a galley before and was curious at the stowage of all the weaponry. Their galley had a full fifty oars which could move them quickly out of the harbour, but the number of soldiers on board was much diminished as it was not expected that these two boats would be engaged with the enemy. They headed out of the harbour with sails still wrapped around the yardarms and under the power of only thirty of their fifty oars.

Francesco was directing the captain of this ship and the alarm was raised as the horizon became darker and more threatening. The oars were soon stowed and sails unfurled to catch the wind. Francesco and the *sopracomito* were hoping to outrun the storm, but instead they were racing directly into the black maw of it.

"Take Desdemona below decks, Emilia. The ship's captain has given over his cabin for your comfort. Stay there and try keep the girl occupied. She has not been on a ship before and this first experience may put her off sailing forever. We are in for a terrific battle with the tempest to our south." He spoke clearly and shouted slightly to rise above what was now a howling wind. The sky overhead, ironically, was bright blue and sunny; but the seas were dark and roiling. White crests began to appear all around on meter high swells. Emilia was in her element. She had grown up with the caprice of the sea and knew not to fight it, but to move with it. Beside her, Desdemona was clutching her shawl with a look of abject terror. The rolling of the ship was causing her to turn pale and Emilia recognized the beginnings of seasickness.

"Quickly. Hold onto my arm and we will get out of this wind, or soon we will be drenched with spray." They struggled aft and scrambled down the narrow gangway to a spacious cabin. The desk occupied the center of the compact space. Carafes of liquor and small cut glass goblets were set into shaped cut-outs on the desktop. The lanterns were seated in hinged baskets that allowed them to remain upright as the ship rolled. Books and navigational instruments lined the low walls on special fortified shelves. Across the back of the cabin was a bowed window of leaded glass panes. The rime of the sea had blurred the view, but the women noticed the pitch and yaw of the boat as the horizon line slid almost vertical and then over righted in the other direction.

"Have you been on a warship before?" Desdemona asked. She was swallowing frequently and Emilia knew this was part of the sickness that would soon lay the girl low.

"I have been on boats all my life." She tried to sound familiar with the situation, but, of course, being on a fishing skiff or a ferry launch was quite different than this galley in a tempest. "Take small sips of water. It will help settle you." She poured a bit of water from the carafe and placed the goblet carefully in Desdemona's hands. "She looks so very young," Emilia thought. "Could I have ever looked so young and been so trustingly naive?"

"Thank you. You are so kind. I am sorry that you had to be brought into this affair. My father was so furious and my loyalty is to my husband now. I wish he were with us on this boat." She closed her eyes a bit. Her skin looked grey and clammy. "Oh, I feel so ill."

"Lay down on the bunk. I will be here next to you." Emilia gently pushed her back on the pillows and helped her slip out of her damp gown, shoes and stockings. The bunk itself was balanced on a gyro to keep it level as the boat rose and fell on the waves like a horse leaping over walls.

Desdemona was ill several times and claimed that she felt better for it. Emilia held a bowl for her and then swabbed her face with a cool damp cloth. Night had fallen, but they had not lit a lantern, as Francesco was afraid that any light could alert enemy ships trailing behind the main fleet.

"Lay with me, Emilia. I am so afraid." Desdemona's teeth were chattering. She was weakened by the seasickness; but she was stiff and alert, convinced that with every groan of the ship's hull or snap of the canvas sails, a mast would crash down on them or the vessel would crack in two.

"Pray with me. I fear we are going to drown in this storm and I will never see my beloved." She began to cry softly. "We had not even had the opportunity to consummate our union before he had to choose the Republic over his bride!" She was feeling sorry for herself and Emilia supposed she had a right to cry a bit. Poor thing.

Emilia recalled her own wedding and the sumptuous feast that followed. Her mother's tears, her father's pride. This young girl was like the orphan she had married. She was alone with no one but her husband to care for her and he was fighting the Turk on a far off shore for the honour of Venice.

"He will have plenty of time to make it up to you, sweet child. Men crave our favours and will not choose the state forever. When he takes you, you will understand. It will be glorious for you both and will bind you together forever." She stroked the girl's cheek and dabbed at her tears with her handkerchief. The lace edge reminded her of her own mother and she was filled with gratitude that she had not lost *her*, as had this poor child.

"Hold me, Emilia. I am so frightened." Emilia took off her heavy gown and the two young women lay side by side in the rocking bunk, holding each other for comfort as the winds went from howling to screaming and the boat seemed to be on its side more often than on its hull.

Neither knew that above decks the men had lashed themselves to various poles and masts to prevent being washed overboard. Navigation had become impossible and they secured the wheel with ropes to a position of a compass reading of due south. They prayed that when the storm had stopped they would be somewhere near their target of Cyprus.

Emilia had dozed, but a crack of lightening woke her with a start. In the pale light of the next flash, she saw that Desdemona's eyes were wide and glassy with fear.

"Desdemona, are you awake?" Emilia wanted to get the girl talking. She seemed to be mute with fear and shock.

"I am awake, but I know not if I be in purgatory, on earth or in hell." She groaned.

"Tell me about your life. What was it like growing up in a grand palace? Your father is a Senator and there must have been many important occasions." Emilia hoped to draw her out.

"Well, mostly I recall being very small and being cared for by my nurse. My father's business took place on the other side of the palace and I rarely saw him, much less any of his important visitors." Desdemona was warming to her story. "My nurse taught me to study well and to respect my father as is my duty to him." Her voice softened to a whisper, "She taught me about becoming a woman and explained all to me."

Emilia was curious to know if this was a universal sort of knowledge – the sort of advice she had heard from her aunts and her mother before her own betrothal and marriage. "What type of advice did your nurse give?"

"She had been married three times. Her first husband died in a duel protecting her honour. Her second died of the plague. Her last and third husband lost his fortune and abandoned her. She was fortunate that my father found her and knew her to be an honest woman. She had raised three sons, one from each of her husbands. They all went to sea as fishers or sailors." Desdemona sighed. "She told me that marrying a sailor, a man of fortune, would be a hard life, but she, too, admired the Moor."

"And her advice to you?" Emilia persisted, more curious than ever to learn the secrets of the nurse.

"She told me that I must offer my favours to my husband without fear or modesty. She told me to pleasure him in every way. She used to fondle me to show how I must lead him to my own treasures and that he would be happy to forsake the sea and hurry back to me each chance he had."

"Hmm. I think that my aunts and mother gave me the same advice, but with more discretion." Emilia was becoming enchanted with this woman child who was innocent and yet sage. "Let us pray that soon we will be united with our husbands on *terrafirma* and can sport with them; and, like sirens, lure them away from duty to our beds."

Desdemona liked this plan and laughed a girlish laugh that had a hint of bawdy bass notes mingled with a crystal tinkling. "To which saint should we direct the prayer?" she asked with a playful tone.

"Amen. To which saint," thought Emilia. "By which miraculous interception can I become the fiery girl who wooed Francesco so long ago?"

"We must offer a prayer to the Virgin, herself, who suffered her Seven Sorrows," Emilia said solemnly. Desdemona squeezed Emilia to her and kissed her warmly on the mouth.

"You are my new friend, Emilia. I am so fortunate to be with you in this trial. My husband chose well when he asked that you accompany me." Desdemona looked deeply into Emilia's eyes in the gloom of the cabin. "Never leave me, dearest one."

Chapter Twenty

$\mathcal{I}$t had been almost a week since her interview with the Tribunal. Stefano and Don Lorenzo took turns coming to visit her, bringing food and news from the outside. There was not much news to report, it seemed. Either that, or most of it involved the scandal and was deemed too unsettling to share with the prisoner.

Then almost two weeks had passed when the guard alerted Emilia to the arrival of her lawyer. Emilia stood to greet Dottore Santacroce.

"Good day, Signora. How are you?" He took off his cape and threw it over one of the chairs. A larger table and three chairs had been permanently moved into the room. The door to the cell was rarely locked and often stood open to allow a fresh breeze to blow across the small stone room. He had not waited for her answer before he launched into a speech, that he had clearly prepared before coming. "Signora, I have some very discouraging news. I know that things seemed to be moving in our favour and that the Inquisitors were almost convinced that you had been duped by your husband, who was the traitor and instigator in the tragedy, but new developments have changed the course of their thinking. May I?" he motioned to the other chair.

Emilia had not placed much credence in the optimism that Santacroce, Stefano and Don Lorenzo had voiced. She had resigned herself to the worst and felt numbed to the actual process which had the men so exercised on her behalf.

"Continue, Dottore. I know how much you have done for me in pleading my case. My appreciation out weighs any possible disappointment in the outcome of the trial." She spoke dispassionately, sitting with hands folded in her lap. She felt tired and somewhat bored with the whole affair. This prison was limbo. At least a decision would mean a change.

"The sad news is that Senator Branbantio has died. His heart was broken by the elopement of his daughter and her death broke his spirit. He has been hanging on to life," he regretted his wording, "ahem, barely living, since news from Cyprus reached Venice." Santacroce shifted in the chair, "Revenge is a terrible passion. It is a corrosive, silent agent that burns, but does not cauterize, a wound." The lawyer shook his head. He knew defeat.

He continued. "This death has cast a further pall on the affair. The man was respected and had many influential friends. His last wish was for his daughter's death to be avenged. He pointed to you as the only living witness or participant in the intrigue. There is heavy pressure on the Council to find you guilty of treason." There. He had said it. It was her death sentence, in so many words. He stared hard into her blank face. He had expected some hysteria; at the very least, he thought she might weep or swoon.

"So be it. I commend myself to God's divine will." Emilia stood and walked the short distance to her cot. She stretched out, closed her eyes and lay very still.

The lawyer was dumbfounded. It was as if she had welcomed the verdict. He stared at the beautiful young prisoner, who now resembled the effigy of a noblewoman on the lid of a sarcophagus. He had been dismissed. He took his cloak and walked slowly out the door.

Emilia found her escape in her memory. She drifted back to the landing in Cyprus and her growing affection for the sweet innocent Desdemona. Their boat landed before Othello's; by some quirk of fate, the winds had blown them past the fleet. On the landing they were greeted by the Michael Cassio – the object of Francesco's disdain: the man made lieutenant in his place.

Emilia noticed the lieutenant's formal manners and thought his effusive greeting to Desdemona was cloying. Francesco burned when Cassio kissed Emilia's cheeks in greeting, but turned his sarcasm inward and outward to his wife and against women in general under the guise of repartee.

"You women are pictures out of doors, bells in your parlours, wild-cats in your kitchens, saints in your injuries, devils being offended, players in your housewifery and housewives in," he paused for effect, "your beds!" Francesco joined the company in laughter at his own appraisal of women.

But Desdemona was clearly offended on Emilia's part by her husband's rudeness and traded quip for quip nearly outdoing Francesco at his own game of hidden insults. Francesco barely took notice of the girl's outspoken retorts. He could barely contain his smouldering anger at Cassio, who was trying to curry favour on both sides. The tension mounted as finally a cry was heard from the harbour. A ship had been sighted.

Othello, victorious, had arrived. Strangely, in the circumstances, the General greeted his young wife before even making an official greeting to his men. Emilia was struck by the immensity of the man's bearing. He looked powerful. As regal as Caesar. He spoke well and formed his words of love to Desdemona with an almost poetic cadence. Emilia had understood from Desdemona's story, that he had been self-educated; and that the Moor had come from a regal line in his own country.

Finally Othello turned to his men and proclaimed officially that the Turks had been vanquished; an end of war called for celebration. He placed his new lieutenant in charge of the company and led Desdemona to their private apartments. Emilia was pleased that the young wife would finally have a proper wedding night with her General. She wished their bed a blessing.

Meanwhile, Francesco had stood a distance apart. The blood in his eye did not match the smile he wore. As Emilia made her way from the harbour she noticed that her husband was in deep conference with a gentleman from Venice who had joined the company.

In fact, there were several hangers-on who had been aboard their ship bound for Cyprus. One of the party was a courtesan who openly professed her love for Michael Cassio to anyone who would listen.

Emilia went to her rooms, which were across a wide corridor from Othello's apartment. Francesco insisted that he would stay in the barracks that night to watch over the men. He wanted to keep a close eye on the young lieutenant, Emilia surmised.

The following day Emilia woke early and discretely knocked on the door of the wedding chamber. She was bid to enter by Desdemona, who was standing at a tall window in her dressing gown. Emilia greeted her and led her to the cushioned bench before the dressing table. She began brushing Desdemona's hair. The young girl was a beauty. Her hair was like pale silk and her features were finely etched, only her chin seemed a bit too pointed; but the viewer's gaze was drawn to the hypnotic grey eyes that fluctuated between the indecision of green or blue. Her thick dark lashes were startling considering her fair colouring. This morning her eyes were lowered and her usual girlish chatter was replaced with a pensive quiet.

"So did your General have his way with you last night, Desdemona?" Emilia kept her tone light. She was merely hoping to get the girl talking and shake her out of her mood.

"Not exactly." Desdemona met Emilia's eyes in the mirror in front of them. "Did you sleep through the uproar last night?"

"I am not an efficient companion, my sweet. I am afraid I fell into a deep and exhausted sleep as soon as I found my bed." Emilia returned her gaze, the brush stopped midway down Desdemona's long, thick hair. "What happened?" Some alarm seemed to be chiming in Emila's heart. "Francesco, what have you done?" she thought.

"It seems young Cassio became aggressively drunk and wounded a man. Othello has relieved him of his office. The poor boy is devastated."

"Oh, God," Emilia dropped the brush. "Who was the man? Is the wound serious?"

"I think Othello said his name," Desdemona pursed her mouth in thought and Emilia was distracted by the effect. The girl was charming in every aspect. "It was Mon... something."

"Montano?" Emilia hazarded a guess. She had heard the name. He was the governor of the island. Relief flooded through her. She had feared the worst.

"I am not sure." Desdemona stood and waved away Emilia's ministrations. "The only thing I know for sure is that this sword fight caused my husband to abandon his marriage bed. And, if you must know, I am still not properly wedded!"

She seemed unconcerned about the man's fate and annoyed with her husband. "Othello took it upon himself to dress the man's wounds and, as a result, has not been back in this chamber since the alarm was raised."

A soft knock was heard at the door and Emilia crossed the room to answer. A servant handed her two notes and motioned to the young mistress.

"Oh, Emilia, can you please read them to me. I am so unhappy and distracted," Desdemona stretched out on the bed and her dressing gown fell open revealing the smooth creamy skin of her neck. She stretched like a long cat and rolled to her stomach tangling her hair around her neck. Her movements were fluid and sensuous. "Please?"

Emilia opened the first note. The curling feminine script was large and yet almost hard to read, it was so ornate. She read: "Bounteous madam, I am your true servant. Can you please plead my suit to your husband to reinstate me? I being absent and my place supplied, I fear my general will forget my love and service. I ask leave to have some brief discourse with you. Ever your devoted, Michael Cassio." Emilia looked up questioningly.

"We will let the young man know that I will plead his case with my husband. I am *sure* I can persuade Othello to reconsider Cassio's place." A sense of purpose seemed to help the young mistress shed her lethargy. The challenge gave her something to try. She shed her dressing gown and quickly began dressing. "Read the second note, Emilia," she called from underneath the gown she was struggling into over her head.

"Gentle Madame, I am in Cyprus, as you are, to be close to one I love. Being familiar with the ways of the island I would like to invite you and your friend to join me at the baths. The Hammam is renown as a place of beauty and repose. Please agree to join me. I will wait for you at the gates of the fortress before noon. B."

"It is the courtesan who is following Cassio," Emilia felt an edge of outrage in her voice. "She is bold to offer to include us in her leisure."

"Not at all, Emilia. I think she is lonely and bored as we are. We should meet her and partake of the traditions of the island. I have read of the Hammam and the sultan's concubines and harem would spend the whole day there being pampered and groomed."

An infectious optimism and liveliness infused her manner. She quickly pinned her hair on top of her head and reached for a shawl, applying it like a veil, as was the custom on the island. "Come. You must join me. It will be amusing." She pulled on Emilia's hand and they both left the chamber to find the fortress gate.

As they walked the perimeter of the fort, they heard a call from the rampart. Othello stood like Ramses at the tower. "There is my husband," Desdemona waved to him and blew him kisses. "He is magnificent." Emilia noted. The General bowed to them and saluted. He seemed pleased that the women had found diversion with each other.

Bianca was a little older than Emilia and experience gave her authority. She led them through the maze of the market, or *souk*, to a domed building. The baths were only opened to women during certain hours of certain days. All the other times, men reigned over the steamy kingdom.

The hot moist air hit Emilia with force. She felt smothered by the waves of heat emanating from the baths. Heavily veiled women led them into an open cubicle and began to help them out of their gowns and slips. The women were handed muslin sheets to wrap in, but were virtually naked. Next they were taken to a small marble chamber where dry heat emanated from the vents in the floor. Above, thin light penetrated the wavy gloom from hexagonal windows that pierced the high domed ceiling.

None of the three could speak. The hot air was so intense it made breathing difficult. Emilia felt a momentary panic, then, all of sudden, it was as if her body opened. Water sprang from every pore and her skin became shiny and slick. She stood in a pool of her own fluid. She felt dizzy from the heat and sat heavily on a stone bench against the wall. Even her scalp was pouring moisture and her hair became heavy with the sweat. Her eyes burned from the salty drops flowing down her forehead.

She looked through the gloom and noticed that Bianca had shed her sheet and was smoothing the drops of perspiration off of her body with her hands. Desdemona had followed her lead and was standing next to her like Eve in a painting of the Garden. Her sheet swaddled on the floor next to her; she was smoothing her shiny, moist skin with her long delicate hands. Emilia let her sheet drop from her shoulders, but held it at her waist. The rosebud breasts of the young mistress looked almost boyish next to the heavy orbs of the courtesan, which swung slowly with the movement of her massage.

Emilia looked down at her own breasts; they were firm, but traced with thin silver lines. Although she had not suckled her daughter, her breasts had swollen painfully from the engorging milk. The wet nurse had helped her expel the milk to ease the pressure, but these lines were reminders that she had given birth. "I am a mother," Emilia thought with a pang of shame at being in this hedonistic Hammam with a courtesan.

Before this thought had taken hold, the three were being led to another small chamber. Here the veiled women sponged them with cool water from deep buckets. Water cascaded from an intricately carved fountain in the wall, spilled to the floor and emptied into a series of ornamental drains. The sheets had been left behind and the veiled women roughly scrubbed all parts of their bodies using sponges heavy with cool water.

The initial shock of the coolness turned to a soothing sensation. Emilia closed her eyes and gave herself over to the veiled woman who was assigned to minister to her. This abruptly ended and once more dry warm sheets were wrapped around the women as they were led to yet another marble chamber.

This time the heat was heavy with steam. Visibility was completely blocked by clouds of thick steam and Emilia again gasped for air. Eventually her lungs seemed to relax and welcome the moist warmth. Hot stones beneath the pierced floor were doused with water to create more clouds of steam. Emilia felt like she was floating in a cloud. Disembodied hands reached out from the cloud to lead her to a long bench. There she was made to lie back and the sheet was opened to allow the steam to reach her body. They stayed the longest in this chamber; finally, Emilia reluctantly allowed herself to be led to the door.

Now they were in the large opened centre of the dome. A series of marble benches were placed head to toe to mirror the hexagonal shape of the opening high above. Each slab had grooves on the edge to act as drains. There were buckets of clear water and sponges positioned at each marble bed.

Emilia was placed face down on the marble bed, lying on thick towelling. A large woman wearing only a loincloth approached the bench and took a puffed bag of coarse muslin that was heavy with soap suds and began to rub briskly and roughly all over Emilia's back and down her legs. No part of her was left untouched as the woman pressed and rubbed and scraped with the sudsy muslin.

Emilia was repulsed to note that the soapy water that ran into the grooved channels was greyish. "This was dirt and filth that has accumulated for all of my twenty one years," she thought with disgust. She recalled all the peremptory baths of her life, standing in a metal basin and using a small sea sponge with soap her mother had made from olive oil. It had served her well enough, she reasoned.

These thoughts were quickly dispelled as she was summarily flipped onto her back like a large fish on the slab. The women brought new muslin and began a gentler, but still vigorous scrubbing. She massaged Emilia's breasts, under her arms, between her legs and down to her feet, which received particular attention with a large smooth pumice stone.

Next a bucket of warm water was poured over her hair and the woman moved her hands in wide circles through Emilia's hair, massaging her scalp in such a way that Emilia moaned with pleasure. The woman was working hard to press on various points at the base of Emilia's skull and bare breasts of the Turkish woman swung heavily right over Emilia's face. Rather than focus on that, Emilia closed her eyes and gave herself over to the treatment.

Soon sponges were emptied over her, rinsing all the soap and grime down the drains beneath the table.

Just when Emilia thought the process had ended, the woman took fistfuls of a paste made from coarse sea salt and olive oil, and began to massage her again. Back first, then her front. The oiliness of the poultice softened her skin and made it shine. She thought of the oiled emery clothes used by the apprentices to polish the marble statues at Salute.

This final treatment ended with more warm, then cool water and another clean sheet. Her knees felt weak as she was led to wood panelled cubicle, where sunlight filtered softly through stained glass windows. Cushioned wooden benches lined the walls and delicate incense filled the air. Emilia was handed a small glass of sweet mint tea. Bianca and Desdemona were already seated and sipping their tea, silently, looking drugged and sleepy. The bath had been invigorating, but the result was a feeling of complete relaxation and lethargy.

Finally, Bianca spoke. "Did you enjoy the Hammam?" she smiled coyly, her pretty round face and small pointed teeth reminded Emilia of a pampered kitten. Bianca's curled hair had wound even more tightly with the damp of the Hammam. It sparkled with red highlights and her skin was so flushed that the sprinkling of freckles that covered her nose and arms were barely visible. Her playful smile belied her age and Emilia could see how men would be drawn to her.

Desdemona was the first to respond. "The baths are wonderful. I have never experienced anything like it and it far surpasses the descriptions in my books about Arabia."

"The first time I visited the Hammam was in Constantinople. The baths there are world-renowned. They even have rooms where men and women can bathe together, but the infidels frown it upon. They require their women to be completely veiled and only their husbands may see even their hands!" Bianca adjusted her sheet to reveal her shoulders. Desdemona stared at her in admiration.

"How did you meet Michael Cassio?" she asked.

"All the sailors visit our district in Venice at one time or another," Bianca looked pointedly at Emilia, who felt her face flush even more than it already was from the bath.

"Michael Cassio was brought by his compatriots as a sort of initiation. He was younger than they and had never been with a woman. I felt honoured to be the one to educate him, so to speak." She smiled gently at Desdemona, clearly pleased to answer the girl's question.

"As I mentioned, all the sailors seek our custom and the Mother Church herself allows us free enterprise in order to discourage liaisons between the sailors on their ships. Although," she said with a certainty, "as much as the men love to visit courtesans, what goes on aboard the ships is well publicized." Desdemona's eyes became wide and she suppressed a shudder.

"Michael Cassio is of a different ilk. He is faithful to me and has restraint and self-discipline, which causes me more puzzlement about the indiscretion of the other night. He has often confessed to me of his poor and unhappy brain for drinking. He was loathe to take even a glass of wine with his dinner. For this reason I cannot credit that he spurned his duty and became drunk the other night. He is devastated by the loss of his office and his reputation."

Bianca looked pointedly at Desdemona, "Anything you can do to persuade your General to reinstate him would be greatly rewarded in his gratitude and in mine." She placed her hand on Desdemona's.

"I will do all in my abilities on his behalf." Desdemona put her other hand on Bianca's to seal her vow. "It is said that you hope he will marry you."

Emilia was shocked at the boldness of Desdemona's questions, but was herself curious to hear Bianca's answer.

"He has led me to believe he is of a mind to do so," her smile widened. "I do love him to distraction and he seems to return my affection." She saw skepticism in Emilia's eyes. "Oh, yes, it is unusual for a courtesan to be made an honest lady by a gentleman. But it is not unheard of."

She looked directly at Emilia with barely disguised scorn. "And you, madam, perhaps you can direct me how I can serve my husband in such a way that he will never seek his pleasures with such as me, when I am his honest wife?"

Emilia had come to accept that with her reluctance to become close to Francesco after Martina's birth, almost certainly he had strayed back to Calle de Tette with his crew. She realized that she had almost welcomed the relief from having to make excuses to avoid her duty. Besides, when she had made overtures to him, he had not seemed interested or able to accept her romantic offerings. But she could not rationalize her failings. No, his sin was a fault of hers and she bore the guilt. She could not blame him. Still, this woman's barbs had hit the mark.

"Bianca, an honest wife?" thought Emilia, "No, she was a common whore and would never be anything else. Michael Cassio would be ensnared in her web if he was not careful,"

Chapter Twenty-One

Venice is an island, as is Cyprus. But Venice is the center of world - the navel of the universe. Cyprus is on the edge of the world; Cyprus is different. Exotic. Anonymous. The women were free to wander and meet. All guard was down. Social stations such as being a Senator's daughter, an Ensign's wife or a courtesan seemed immaterial. There were no boundaries. Perhaps it was the song of the palm trees, which whispered in evening under starry nights. Maybe it was the sirocco, which blew in the afternoon driving them all to their chambers for lingering siestas. Sensations were heightened. It was Mediterranean.

The Hammam had set the tone. Languid. The dry heat of day and cool moisture of the night instilled sensuality. Clothing became lighter out of doors and insignificant in the confines of the chamber. Desdemona still yearned for her husband to behave like a husband and less like a general, but he had shown her little consideration since the first days of their arrival. In fact, he even seemed to be growing increasingly angry and resentful toward her. This puzzled the young bride and caused her to lean more and more on Emilia for consolation, advice and affection.

The two women took long walks in the early coolness of the day and lay for hours in the curtained bed, reading to each other, discussing the mysterious world of men and deciding that a woman's world was safer, simpler and more secure. They slept the long, hot afternoon hours entwined in each other's arms and woke to dress and groom each other for the promenade that would lead into the long late suppers in the governor's court.

Finally Emilia had the opportunity to speak with Francesco in private. She had something he wanted and would use it to lure him to her. Something about the atmosphere of the warm island had awakened feelings in her that had long been dormant. She yearned to be held by him, to be loved again. When he came to her chamber she noticed slight changes in him – his manner, even his smell. He did not smell like the island, but like the oils of the ship and the bitterness of the sweat of fear.

"I have missed you these days. Are you happy now that Cassio has been dismissed from his position as Lieutenant?" She moved close to her husband and kissed him on each cheek and gently on his mouth. He did not respond, but seemed distracted as he walked to the arched window and leaned heavily on the casement. "If only things were as uncomplicated as that, Emilia." He sighed deeply and stared into the sharp afternoon light. "Othello does not recognize my worth. His offence is still fresh to me; therefore, no, I am not *happy*, as you say. I am not content and fear I will never again be so." He turned and she saw the emptiness in his eyes. He looked aged and spent. "My darling!" Emilia held him and tried to console him. He stood stiffly with his arms at his sides, not returning her embrace. "Please, husband, I know I have not been a wife to you for a long time, but I have never stopped loving you." She stroked his damp curls, hoping to feel some stirring in his body, some sign that he could be reached. "Why did you call me to your chamber, Emilia?" He broke out of her embrace. "I cannot be away from the barracks for too long."

Emilia assumed a dignified air. "Once you asked me a favour and I called you to me to bestow it." Francesco looked more annoyed than intrigued. "Well?" he demanded.

"I have the token you asked me to secure from Desdemona – the handkerchief. Now that Othello is so displeased with her, she has become more careless and dropped it on the floor. Knowing how much you wished to have it, I retrieved it and now I bring it to you." Emilia produced the delicate square of cloth from her sleeve and held it toward him. Francesco stepped toward her with his hand outstretched. Emilia thought his face betrayed a wicked glee. She quickly whipped the handkerchief behind her back. "But you must pay for this favour with one of your own."

"Do not toy with me, Emilia. I have no time for this nonsense." He looked almost menacingly at her.

"The stuff of our love is not nonsense, my dear. I am serious when I say that I want to renew our closeness and this occasion can mark the first step." She reached for him and kissed him deeply, wrapping her arms around his neck and leading him to the couch. Francesco returned the pressure of her kisses and reached up to the front of her gown. His hands felt rough and awkward, but it seemed only to make Emilia more aware of the urgency of her mission to woo him back to her. "What would the courtesan do?" she wondered. She took his hand from her bodice and deftly unfastened the clasps herself. Stepping out of her light gown, she stared straight into his eyes with a bold defiance. Preparing for her battle she had armoured herself in a short transparent slip which revealed her shape. Francesco's eyes were drawn to the dark shadow between her legs and then up to her rosy nipples, which strained against the fragile silk. He seemed aroused by his wife's new boldness. Emilia watched the barometer of his face for signs that she had won this skirmish. She looped the small handkerchief around his neck like a lacy garrotte and drew his head down to her breasts. His warm breath came in short gasps and he reached for her.

She had delivered the token Othello had given his wife: the handkerchief. She had no idea of Francesco's plan for it. She only wanted to please him in some way to make up for her own lapses – and perhaps to soothe her own conscience which wrestled with her growing feelings for Desdemona. At any rate, Francesco took the napkin and left her chamber puzzled, yet sated, by his wife's passion.

Emilia was washing herself at the basin when a soft knock at the door signalled that Desdemona had returned from her walk with Cassio. She looked flushed and uncomfortable. Her distractions were understandable considering Othello's continued aggression towards her. Emilia wrapped a light robe over her nakedness and anointed her neck with bergamot oil.

"Come, sit." Emilia motioned to the silk covered pillows piled on the cool tiles of the marble floor. Desdemona shed her outer cape and sank into the soft pillows stretching her arms over her head. Her face looked drawn and sad. Emilia knelt down beside the distracted girl. She gently rolled her onto her stomach and began to knead the knots that had formed between Desdemona's shoulders, releasing some of the tension held there.

"How did your interview with Michael Cassio progress?"

"He is very sweet, but feels that he is isolated in the fortress. His only friend at this point, oddly enough, is Iago. They are sharing a room in the barracks and Michael is taking advice from your husband on how to proceed." The young mistress moved slightly to offer resistance to the pressure of Emilia's massaging hands. Emilia could feel the girl relaxing. Desdemona turned her head, "And you? How was your interview with Iago?" She smiled and for a moment Emilia remembered Bianca's sly smile in the baths.

"He is like a caged mongoose, wishing for a chance to fight the cobra, as usual. He always seems to be in the state of readiness for a battle and when he does not have one, he becomes unbearable. It is as if I can see the mechanism behind his eyes and the cords tightening. He has become so strange." Emilia's hand paused in her task as she mused about her husband's state of mind.

Desdemona squirmed to encourage Emilia to continue the massage, "Perhaps it is the island air. Both of our men seem melancholy and anxious." Desdemona may have hit on the cause. She rolled onto her back. "Now let me massage you. Your skin is flushed and perfume is musky. Did you make love with your husband in the afternoon heat?" She playfully pulled Emilia down to her as if to wrestle with her. "Oh, how I wish my General would come to me in the afternoon." Emilia closed her eyes and allowed the massage to commence. She emptied her mind of Francesco and concentrated only on the sensation of the smooth, cool hands working on her muscles.

"Emilia, can you braid my hair in that intricate way?" Desdemona was in front of her dressing table lifting long ropes of her spun gold hair. She twisted it into coils around her head and then let it fall down her back.

"Of course, dear one. I love brushing your hair. It is so soft and thick. It has a texture that is so different from my own." Emilia stood behind her and took up a silver backed brush. She watched the reflection of Desdemona's face as she began sweeping the brush in long strokes through the girl's hair. Desdemona closed her eyes and her mouth curled slightly up at the edges. She seemed to purr with contentment at Emilia's light touch.

"Did you hear that a ship from Venice arrived today," Emilia began to separate the long hair into columns, which she would then twist and secure into braids of different widths.

"Yes. I know. It brought my uncle and cousin from the Senate. I wonder if they have news from my father. I hope that he is not still angry with me for my deception." Desdemona opened her eyes to see if Emilia had an insight on this matter.

"I feel so far from Venice. It seems that matters of the Republic can hardly touch us here. Do not fret." She opened an intricately carved sandalwood box, lifting out clumps of tangled necklaces and jewels. She chose strings of pearls, delicately separating them from the mass, picking rosy pearl strands to weave into the braids.

"I wish my husband were kind to me. I fear that our marriage will be dissolved somehow if he does not make me his true wife." The consummation of their union was the only way she could defy any move to annul the marriage. Emilia felt the girl's fears were unfounded. It would be widely assumed that she and Othello were securely joined by now. However, it did seem odd to Emilia that the General had not been anxious to try his new wife.

"I am sure that Brabantio has accepted that you are the wife of his honoured General and the concerns of the Republic have moved on to other pressing matters." She pinned the final braids in place and stepped back to view her handiwork. A thick coil circled the top of Desdemona's head and smaller braids were looped and secured to look like delicate hoops of gold chain hanging from the crown. Emilia had entwined the strands of pearls and the whole effect was elegant but sweetly innocent. "There. What do you think?" Emilia stood next to the girl who was holding a mirror to view the entire picture – back and front.

"It is splendid. You are an artist, Emilia." They moved together to the cupboard and began to choose which gown would complete the effect. Emila watched Desdemona pull one dress and then another out of the closet. She laid them on the bed and pondered which would suit. Emilia felt a rush of affection for her and put her arms around Desdmona's shoulders. They fell onto the heaped gowns, laughing, and clung tightly to each other. Desdemona kissed Emilia warmly and pulled her tightly to her. Emilia did not know if her breathlessness was from the strong embrace or the gentle kisses. She felt tears behind her eyes aching to be shed.

"I wish we did not have to go to the court tonight. I may tell my husband that I am not well," Emilia dreaded seeing Francesco so out of sorts. Outwardly he behaved as the loyal and contented ensign, but she could see the simmering fury in his eyes. It made her feel ill to think of how dangerous he seemed these days. "I wish I could stay here in this tangle of silk, in this chamber, with you forever." Emilia buried her face in Desdemona's bosom and sighed deeply.

Desdemona disengaged herself from Emilia and stood at the foot of the bed. "I *must* go to dinner. It may be the only time I have to be close to my husband today. Perhaps when he sees me he will soften and change the mood he is in lately." She was already stepping into a gown. In moments she had been transformed from the dreamy girl lying with Emilia on the bed, to an elegant, composed Venetian woman ready to join the court.

"You are right, of course. He needs only to see you and he will fall under your spell." Emilia kissed Desdemona lightly on her cheeks and draped a lacy shawl across her shoulders. The gold braid trim on the pale silk gown repeated the braids of hair. "You are so beautiful tonight." Emilia felt overcome with tenderness for the girl. It was a mixture of love, protectiveness and some other emotion she could not quite place, but there was a tinge of guilt overriding the whole of it. "Perhaps these are the feelings I should have for little Martina," her mind once more shifted to her lapsed responsibilities to her tiny vulnerable daughter. Or were these feelings she had once felt for him – her Ensign?

At court Emilia remained a spectator. From the colonnaded loggia she watched all eyes turn to her darling, Desdemona. All eyes, except Francesco's. His eyes remained riveted on the General. Emilia recognized the familiar blaze of hellfire hidden in his stare. The minor keys of the local musicians seemed soothingly foreign to the visitors from Venice. There was no news of Brabantio, but a change of government was heralded in a letter from the Doge. Othello was needed back in Venice. Cassio would be left to govern Cyprus. Othello's rage at this news evoked irrational babbling and violence toward his most loyal subject. Emilia gasped and barely prevented herself from intervening when Othello struck Desdemona, knocking her down – seemingly for no reason. No one in the court was more amazed than Desdemona's uncle and cousin who stared in horror. Francesco rationalized the insult and reassured them and the other guests. The General was susceptible to such periods of distraction. He explained that the alien Moor was an enigma.

The climax of that evening marked a tragic denouement to the whole Cyprus victory. Things seemed to revert back to the routine, but the undercurrent of impending doom was stronger. A sort of desperation infused the normal comings and goings of the fortress. Cassio met with Desdemona frequently to ply his suit; and though she approached her husband repeatedly, Othello spoke in riddles and accused her of unknown indiscretions. He seemed unwilling to hear any recommendations for the fallen lieutenant's reinstatement. "Besides," thought Emilia,

"Michael Cassio was to be the new governor of Cyprus. What did he need of Othello's favour?"

When Emilia broached the subject of Othello's rash behaviour to Francesco, he feigned ignorance. "Is my lord angry?" He claimed that he had noticed no change in Othello's demeanour toward Desdemona.

Desdemona made her own excuses for Othello's impatience and strange mutterings. "Sometimes men, who have grave matters on their minds, release their anger on the trivial." She pondered further, "No, we must not think of men as gods or look to them for perfection in their domestic duties. I have been unfair to him to consider his unkindness to be against me. He has much on his mind. I have indicted him falsely." She seemed to be persuading herself to believe this logic.

"His duty is heavy *and* he has been called back to Venice, it is true." Emilia tried to console the young mistress.

Desdemona waved her hand listlessly, "Perhaps he is jealous?" Othello had chided her and publicly shamed her, "But I never gave him cause," she looked pleadingly to Emilia for agreement on this point.

"But jealous men will not be answered so," Emilia reasoned. "They are not ever jealous for a cause, but jealous *because* they are jealous. It is a monster begot upon itself." Emilia knew only too well the irrational nature of jealousy in her own husband.

Desdemona caught her breath, "Heaven keep that monster from Othello's mind!"

Emilia's pity for the girl turned to anger at Othello and toward men in general. "Before long men show us their true natures. They are all but stomachs and we all but food. They eat us hungrily, and when they are full, they belch us."

"It seemed he was surprised, but not displeased our first night together when I showed him my devotion. Do you think he felt I was too forward?" She looked beseechingly to Emilia. "To call me..." she could not bring herself to say the word. She looked down and sighed, "O, these men, these men."

"We are the injured in this world. It amazes me that we are so loyal and pure; they drive us away from them. Yet, they are free to ignore us and pour *our* treasure into foreign laps," Emilia recalled Bianca's claims. "Or else they break out in peevish jealousies, throwing restraint upon us;" Emilia shuddered and dropped her voice, "or even strike us." She recovered herself, "Shall I go fetch your night-gown?"

"No, unpin me here." Desdemona held Emilia's hand to her shoulder. The young girl looked up into Emilia's eyes with a sorrow that seemed bottomless.

Emilia wished there were something she could do to help her. "I wish you had never seen him!" She began to take Desdemona's hair down gently and tenderly.

Desdemona reached up and held Emilia's hands in hers, "No, I love him so much that even his stubbornness, his checks, and his frowns have grace and favour." Emilia looked with concern at the girl. She was besotted and would allow further cruelties from the man she thought she so loved.

"Please, Emilia, unpin me now. I must be ready when he returns. Tonight he will prove me his wife. I hope that I do not displease him." She touched a sweet exotic ointment to her arms. It was one given to her by an island woman. And she hummed a gentle ballad. Emilia prepared the bed, as she had been asked to do, with the bride's wedding sheets. They were pristine, attesting to the chaste and interrupted evenings Desdemona had spent waiting for her husband to set aside his duty to the Republic and attend to his duty in this chamber.

Desdemona wore the nightgown that Emilia fetched from the wedding trousseau. It was white, an almost transparent linen, trimmed with a green embroidered vines dotted with small red pomegranates, symbols of fertility. After Emilia lowered it over the girl's head,

Desdemona grasped Emilia around her waist and buried her head in Emilia's neck.

"Oh, sweet friend. Stay with me and keep me company. I feel such dread tonight. I fear Othello believes I have been unfaithful to him. Can there be wives who would abuse their husbands in such gross kind?"

"No doubt there are, Desdemona. In Venice it is *known* that wives take lovers. They have their dalliances and go to confessors at the end of every week. But God, is not so easily deceived as are their husbands." Emilia led her to the bed and pinned back the curtains with the silken cords. "Women have appetites, Desdemona, and affections and frailties, as do their men."

Desdemona pulled Emilia down beside her. "Lay with me as we did to ride out the tempest." The girl stroked Emilia's cheek. "You comfort me, my dearest friend. Stay with me." Emilia lay beside her as they had lain during their afternoons of repose. The mixture of sensations Emilia felt was difficult to define. The young girl inspired a maternal protectiveness that even her own daughter had not evoked in her. There was sensuousness in Desdemona's touch that was gentler and more moving than even Francesco's caresses from their first year of love. And then there was something else; there was the frisson of danger – of the forbidden.

"And your kind nurse, what would she advise to kindle passion in your General tonight, my sweet?" Emilia slipped her hand beneath the subtle fabric of the gown. "Would you touch him so?" She placed her palm over Desdemona's navel and gently pressed.

"She would advise that I put his hand here and mine on his strongest, most delicate part," she moved Emilia's hand to rest lower and Emilia sensed the warmth emanating from that sweet place. Desdemona shifted slightly and moaned; the candle on the nightstand flickered in the gentle breeze from the long windows. Palms and mimosas swayed and exuded the perfume of the night. There were flowers on this island, tightly closed in the day that bloomed and opened in the moonlight to breathe their secrets. Desdemona hummed and stroked Emilia's inner arm in cadence to the sad melody. Desdemona paused in her song and in her soft touch. Emilia had almost dozed off in the quiet comfort and warmth of the girl's slim body.

"Who is it that knocked?" Desdemona sat upright, alert.

"It is the wind, my child, only the wind."

Chapter Twenty-two

Emilia awoke. It was not the wind that woke her. It was the General knocking and entering the chamber. Dismissing her. Beside her Desdemona was sleeping; her gentle breath was puffing out her lips and her eye lashes fluttered in her dream.

Emilia did as she was told, but stayed close to the door in the hallway, listening. Desdemona had felt a foreboding and so did Emilia. The Moor still had threat in his demeanor; all the thick cords of muscle in his neck and arms attested to his state – a readiness for battle or for violence.

Echoing in the courtyard were the revelries and shouts from the sailors. It seemed that midnight and midday had no distinction on the island. The narrow streets surrounding the fortress and the fortress itself were teeming with people: vendors, courtesans, sailors gambling, singing, wrestling. The quiet of the chambers usually provided respite, but tonight the quiet was ominous.

Emilia heard voices. No - a voice. The Moor was muttering to himself. She heard the rasp of metal and the clank of his armour. He was preparing for bed. The soft voice continued and Emilia strained to make out what he was saying.

"...Justice break her sword!...One more. One more...and this is the last."

Suddenly Emilia felt guilty at this eavesdropping. He was probably going to make love to his child-wife tonight and Emilia was tending on the voyeuristic, standing like a low servant listening at the door. She turned to leave and go to her own bedroom. Then the tenor of the voice changed and Emilia was drawn back to her post.

It was Desdemona's sweet, soft voice. "..what may you mean by that?" Emilia could just make out the words. The bass of his response and then again the treble of hers. "...killing?...Have mercy on me!" The hairs on Emilia's arms and neck rose up; every fiber of her being went on guard. What should she do?

"Peace, and be still!" Othello whispered in a shout. Emilia could discern the words more clearly now. They were arguing.

"You gave the handkerchief to Cassio," he growled the accusation and yet there was hurt in his voice, a tone of regret.

"No, by my life and soul!" Desdemona was pleading. Emilia thought she might faint. She knew where that handkerchief had gone. She knew where she had placed it. And from there? "Oh, Francesco, what have you done? What have you done?" Her mind was racing and fear rose in her throat. She wanted to burst into the room and confess. She wanted to rescue Desdemona from this dangerous, unreasoning man.

"...never loved Cassio...I never...", her voice was pleading.

"By heaven, I saw my handkerchief in his hand!" Othello's voice rose then lowered,"...murder, which I thought a sacrifice..."

Emilia froze. "Murder! Oh, God. Oh, God." Her hand was on the door handle, but she seemed unable to move, to act. Then she heard a cry.

"O...What, is he dead?" Desdemona cried out and then muffled weeping could be heard, "...I am undone!"

Emilia ran to the end of the corridor. One of the watchmen caught her as she rounded the corner. "Madame. What is the matter? Have you heard of the murder? Don't fear. You are safe here in this quarter." Emilia felt she would faint. "Yes, madame, Michael Cassio has killed a young Venetian; in self defence as I heard it. We are blessed that our new leader, Cassio, though wounded, is safe."

From the end of the hall, Emilia heard a crash of furniture. She left the guard and rushed back to the chamber door in time to hear an angry growling curse. "…strumpet!"

More noise of movement and struggle. The Moor did not try to lower his voice and said with slow and determined cadence, "It is too late."

Emilia pushed at the door, turning the handle proved useless and she began to pound on the thick wood. "My lord, my lord!" He did not respond but continued to mumble. "Please, I would speak to you. Please let me in." Emilia sensed he would not.

Finally she heard his heavy steps coming toward the door. He unlocked it and was outlined in the darkness of the room by the moonlight which streamed through the tall arched window. A wind had risen. The sirocco – the driving wind from the desert that carried the fine red sand which filled every crevice;

the wind was said to drive humans and animals mad. "What is the matter, Emilia?"

"My lord, Cassio has killed a young man. Cassio is wounded. There is a disturbance in the fortress. You must come." She wanted to draw his attention to the commotion in the courtyard and away from her dear one.

"Cassio is killed?" Othello seemed not to understand what Emilia was saying.

She looked beyond the Moor and noticed a rustling behind the curtained bed. She thought she heard a soft cry. "What is that? My lady?" she rushed to the bed and grabbed the curtain pulling it down, not heeding the tearing of the thin fabric. She saw Desidemona lying across the bed. Her face was as pale as the virginal gown she wore, but her lips looked blue and sick.

"Help! Help! Sweet Desdemona! Oh, sweet mistress, speak! Who has done this?" She lifted Desdemona's lips to her ear and the girl whispered hoarsely, "Nobody; I myself. Farewell." Her eyes brimmed with tears.

Emilia heard a wailing cry and realized it was her own anguish that made that mournful noise. Then her body arched with anger and she turned with her teeth bared to Othello. He took a step back,

"She's a liar. I killed her. She's gone to burn in hell for her sins." He was enraged.

Emilia strode up to him, her face near his, "O, she is an angel and you the black devil!"

"She was false. Her adultery with Cassio is well known. Ask your husband. He knew all." He crossed his arms over his magnificent chest and stood his ground.

"My husband!" Emilia could not believe what she heard. "My husband?"

"He, woman, honest Iago," the Moor revelled in his justification, although Emilia sensed a deep sadness behind his bravado.

"She was pure. Her sin was her devotion to her filthy bargain," Emilia spat the words in his face. "You were not worthy of her."

"Peace. You would be wise to stay quiet." He turned and retrieved his sword from the scabbard and stack of armour he had shed on the couch.

"Your sword can only save me from the suffering I feel. I have no concern for my life and I will make your foul deed known." Emilia rushed to the open door screaming murder. "The Moor has killed my mistress! He has killed Desdemona! Murder…"

She ran headlong into Montano, Gratiano and Francesco who were coming into the chamber. She fell into Iago's arms. "Tell them you did not engineer this. Tell the Moor," she sobbed. "I know you could not be so evil. Please tell them," she swung her arm to include the company.

But Francesco could not deny and so he stayed with his story of Desdemona's faithless, immoral acts, despite Emilia's hysterical cries. Too late to stop her mouth, he stabbed her. At first she thought he had struck her a blow in her stomach to knock the wind out of her voice. It felt more like a blow than a wound, but she knew it was a mortal blow.

She dragged herself to the bed and stretched out next to Desdemona. She buried her face in the loose golden hair and breathed the scent of her loved one in her final breath.

Chapter Twenty-three

*B*ut it was not to be her final breath and now she was in the Piombi preparing for that final breath, not the soft dry heat of Cyprus in the perfumed chamber of the bride, but the moist sea air of Venice. A chill and familiar wind.

"The handkerchief!" Emilia sat up, startled out of her reverie, or was it a dream. Had she been asleep? "Oh, God, why did I obey him? The jealousy he spawned in Othello was his own monster, his own master, which had twisted him and destroyed everything. Jealous of my friendship with Dario, the unknown 'lover' at Arsenale. Jealous of the favour the General gave to the young sweet Cassio. Jealous of the pure love between the General and the girl, which, if you only knew, my husband, was flawed. Jealousies born of your own unfounded insecurities, my love; you, who were so perfect and capable and loving. All gone. All gone."

Emilia stood and paced her cell, tears falling from her eyes. "Oh, Francesco, you had no need. You had no need to be jealous." She wondered if he had confessed before his execution. He was so twisted in his own intrigue and in his own false pride at entwining everyone in his plan, that he went to his death and his damnation in one moment. She was sure he had not been repentant. He had been wounded and betrayed and so he struck out. He felt justified.

"You had no need to engineer the death of Desdemona. No need. You killed me then, without even drawing your dagger. I had only hoped to die beside my sweet girl, not live on without her." Emilia sat heavily on the cot exhausted and weeping.

Don Lorenzo found her thus when the guard directed him into the cell. He had come, as he had feared he must short weeks before when he left Chioggia with the sacrament and oils. He would administer the Last Rites.

"My angel, the Council has sent down the verdict. They found the prisoner guilty of treason against the Republic." He sat next to her on the cot and pulled her to him. I am here to help you, my child. Don't weep. God will take you to him."

A calm settled over her as she realized the ordeal was almost over. "Don Lorenzo, she lied in her last breath to save the Moor. She claimed that he had not killed her. Is she damned by that lie?" Emelia looked to him with hope and sadness.

"God knows when a sin is committed for personal gain, treachery, or spite. It sounds to me like the girl lied for love. She forgave the Moor. For this reason, I cannot help but believe that she was saved. She was pure and innocent in every way, no?" he was still holding Emilia under the mantle of his arm, beside her on the cot.

"The vile rumours against her name are the *true* lies. She was honest and pure." Anger tinged Emilia's voice.

"There it is. Our God is merciful and all knowing." He stood and helped her up. "We have some work to do, Emilia," as he began to unpack his small case and set the instruments of his office on the plain wooden table. He kissed the small purple cross embroidered the nape of his stole and put it over his head around his neck, reverently justifying the two ends which were sewn with symbols in gold thread: the sign of the fish and the letters IHS. Next he set small cruets of oil and a bottle of blessed water on a small white linen cloth. The cloth was edged in an intricate lace that incorporated small crosses and chalices in the design. Emilia recognized her own hand in the worked lace pattern. "I have come full circle," she thought. "I am going home."

She knelt on the planked floor beside Don Lorenzo as he made the sign of the cross over her head.

"Bless me, Father, for I have sinned..." She unabashedly told the details of her role in the intrigue. She listed impure and unkind thoughts she had in the Hammam. And thought of all the sins of omission she had committed in her life and particularly in the week on the island of Cyprus. Finally, she could no longer delay the heaviest sin she carried.

"Don Lorenzo, I have been unfaithful to my husband. I have been impure in thought and deed. I want to confess. I am contrite, I believe, but I am not certain. Can I be absolved?"

"Daughter of Christ, think hard on your sins. God knows all and knows your heart. Whatever indiscretion you have committed against the Sixth Commandment must be addressed. If you are to make a good Act of Contrition and be absolved, you must consider how your actions have offended God."

"Not to excuse myself, Father, but I think that my guilt for falling out of love with my husband and my inability to completely take my daughter to my heart, clouded my judgement. All the love I should have given to my family, I gave to the young mistress in my care. I gave her what rightly belonged to Francesco and what naturally should have been in my heart for Martina. Desdemona became both of them to me; she, in return, gave me what she had hoped to give the Moor. This union became a final chance for me to show and feel love." Emilia paused.

"Go on, my child," the priest prompted.

"I am not contrite for loving her, but I am sorry that I did not love my husband and daughter enough."

"If indeed your love was profane, that sin needs full acknowledgement and contrition in order for absolution." Don Lorenzo was gentle but adamant. "However, *agape*, or pure, platonic, altruistic love is another thing altogether. That is the highest form of love."

"I am not so proud as to attempt to justify my sin by calling it a higher, purer love. It was a sin of the flesh. I am truly sorry for having offended God with my profanity and for the selfish cravings of my flesh. I regret I cannot go back and prove a better wife to my husband and mother to my daughter. I have failed."

"My child, do not be so hard on yourself. You are made in the image and likeness of God, and you have been given two gifts, which set you apart from the beasts: free will and intellect. We are not infallible and we struggle in our lives to attain grace and resist temptation. Your life has been a model of goodness and God will reward you. And now, make an Act of Contrition and I will give you my absolution as is in my power invested by God."

The prayer came to her as she had said it all through her life. But rather than a recitation that was almost by rote, it took on a deeper meaning for Emilia this time. This last time.

When Emilia stood, she helped the priest to his feet. The uneven floor had hobbled them and their knees were numbed.

"When?" Emilia asked.

"Tomorrow morning," was his sad reply. "I will sit with you tonight. Stefano plans to come to visit later. He brings news from Chioggia. You parents could not bring themselves to witness you here or stand by at..." his words trailed off. In her mind Emilia finished his sentence, "the execution." Her mind hit on strange unrelated events from her life. But still when she closed her eyes she saw the limp form of her beloved

Desdemona draped across the wedding sheets, her grey-green eyes filled with tears that never fell.

"I will say my Penance," Emilia stretched out on her cot once more and closed her eyes.

Chapter Twenty-four

$\mathcal{D}$ario worked quietly in the seclusion of the loft. Most of the carpenters had left for the day. Those who were still busy had moved their work to the Piazzetta, but he pushed this thought out of his head. He needed to finish wrapping the last figure in quilted cloth and straw before he put it in the crate to be shipped across the Bacino to San Giorgio. This was the most precious and he felt most proud of the way it had turned out.

He had finished his commission in time and already his patron had given him a list of further figures to begin for a new project. He had made his name. There was a sense of accomplishment and triumph in that, but also Dario felt the deep sadness that it had all come too late for him. Like Tancredi the troubadour who wooed his beloved noblewoman, Dario had not been able to gain his honour in time to be worthy of Emilia. The pledge he had made with the *bocolo* six years before still stood: he loved her and would always love her.

With a sigh, Dario began to pound the thick edged nails into the crate. It had taken him the longest to decide on how to complete this statue, but he was satisfied with the result. As Emilia had said, his work would outlive them both and make this world more beautiful and gentle.

From her cell Emilia, Stefano and Don Lorenzo could make out the hollow pounding of the *marangoni* who were at work below in the Piazzetta. Between the two columns, one supporting the statue of winged lion of St. Mark and one the pedestal for St. Thomas, heavy beams were being joined and a planked platform was being erected. This was the traditional site for execution. The carpenters' work was made easier by the luminous full moon that was rising in the east, chasing the sun as it was slowly setting. The two orbs of light seemed to cast an ominous glow through the small leaded window of the cell.

The three were talking softly and had taken light refreshment. Stefano looked weak and haggard. Don

Lorenzo was moving a rosary slowly through his fingers as he spoke.

"I will be sure to keep a close watch on little Martina, Emilia. She is so like you were as a child – lively, inquisitive, and, of course, stubborn," he smiled weakly and held her hand in his. "Do not fear. God is with you."

"Strangely, Don Lorenzo, I feel at peace," she looked down at her hands which still glistened from the holy oil he had used to anoint her. The priest had made a small cross with oil on her ears, eyes, nose, mouth and her hands – the base of all the senses, which are the sources of temptation or sin. It was for this anointing that the sacrament was called Extreme Unction. She had been cleansed and absolved and was in the state of grace.

"I am still incredulous. How can this be happening? Where is justice?" Stefano threatened to break down again.

"Be strong, my brother. It is for the best. I am ready. Please, trust me," she walked to the chair where he was slumped in resignation and disbelief. She knelt down before him. "You must be strong. It is up to you now, Stefano. You *are* the family now. Everyone will look to you, my sweet. Be strong."

He knew she was right, but he felt so alone. Adrift. His father was reduced to a vague old man who could barely speak. Faustina had carried on the household on the island. She was the real source of strength. He had lost all interest in the business, which virtually could run itself with the men he had appointed in charge. "What is the use?" he mumbled.

The hours dragged on. Soon the pounding had stopped; call and response signalled the raising of the scaffolding with thick ropes and wenches. It had been a while since anyone had been executed in the Piazzetta. Don Lorenzo wondered if a crowd would gather to witness the spectacle of a woman put to death for treason. It seemed ludicrous. Still, the Council had decreed.

All sounds from the square stopped. There was not a breath of air and within the cell the two men dozed. Emilia had encouraged Stefano to stretch out on the cot. He seemed so frail and sad. Almost immediately she noticed his breathing even out as he slept. Don Lorenzo had rested his head on the table and the rosary had softly slipped from his fingers.

Emilia stepped into the corridor and walked quietly past the sleeping guard. In the wider part she could look out and down from a larger window which faced the entry to the harbour. Far down she could make out the scaffold in the gloom, standing like a feeble insult between the two magnificent columns. Beyond were tiny lights on boats in the Bacino and further out, stronger lights which emanated from San Giorgio. It made her think of Dario and his figures. Dear Dario. She said a prayer for him, her dearest friend.

Looking straight down, Emilia puzzled at the odd reflections on the stones of the Piazzetta. Then, it struck her: the *aqua alta*, the high water. The heavenly bodies had conspired to bring this phenomenon on this day and Emilia smiled to herself.

"Any intrepid thrill seeker who ventures out at dawn to see the infamous whore of Babylon receive her just desserts will have to wade to the spectacle – or swim," she thought with irony. And, she? Would her body drop through the trap on the scaffold only to float back up to the crossbeam? "No. They have ways of weighting the prisoner to ensure a clean death," she reasoned. "Practice yields perfection, in these and in all matters."

She wandered back to her cell as the first rosy rays of dawn broke through clouds in the East.

Epilogue

*D*on Lorenzo stepped onto the landing and Fra Paolo held him in a close embrace. He had not seen his old friend in almost two years. Lorenzo made the journey to San Giorgio for the dedication of the new library. He wanted to share in Paolo's triumph and celebration. Lorenzo knew what a trial the process of the construction had been for the monk. Now Longhena's design had fulfilled its promise. The structure was magnificent.

"Thank you, dear friend. Thank you for making the journey. I know how reluctant you are to leave Chioggia these days," Paolo took Lorenzo's arm and led him to the dormitory that had been a refuge two years earlier. The walk down the long corridor of monks' cells sent a chill of memory through Lorenzo's mind. It had taken all of his strength to overcome the urge to create an excuse that would allow him to avoid this event.

"Ah, the old haunts. I know how much the ceremony tomorrow will mean for you, Paolo. I would not have missed it." Lorenzo laboured to sound enthusiastic. "I understand that many dignitaries will be on hand, both clerical and secular. It will bring honour to you and the monastery."

"Frankly, Lorenzo, I hope that the exhaustion and relief I feel don't show on my face tomorrow. As much as I have yearned for the completion to the project, I feel I can hardly enjoy it." The monk shook his head slowly. "Plus my eyes see all the flaws and know all the deceptions in the building."

"You are too pessimistic. Only God can create perfection and yet even He chooses to allow flaws in his creations." Lorenzo spoke consolingly, but also sensed the brother was offering a humble view of what Lorenzo knew would be a magnificent feat of architecture and art, as well as a suitable vault to contain the many priceless manuscripts and records of knowledge.

"Thank God, we were spared the damage that was suffered in Venice two years ago with the floods. It could have set us further behind schedule than we already were in completion. What a disaster that was, no?"

"Paolo, do you forget that the night of the *aqua alta* was a particular disaster for me?" Lorenzo felt impatient, but recovered himself. Each of the men had had their own trials in that period: Paolo had the problems with the labourers and artisans. Lorenzo had the tragedy of his Emilia.

"I beg your pardon, friend. How callous of me! Of course, that night was devastation of a different sort in your parish and in your heart." Paolo had halted in the corridor and turned to Lorenzo. "I know the memory of that night has weighed heavily upon you, dear friend. For this reason I appreciate even more your presence here for my small moment of triumph."

"No, no, Paolo. I am too sensitive. God's will be done. My Emilia is with him. I need to rejoin the world of the living, for my parishioners' sakes, if not for decency's sake." Lorenzo felt old and useless. Paolo turned the round ring on the wooden door and escorted Lorenzo into the cell. It contained a cot, chair, desk and washstand.

Above the bed was a simple wooden crucifix and over the desk was a delicate fresco depicting a scene from Christ's passion – the deposition from the cross. The two Marys were standing by, mourning the limp figure of Christ who was being lowered by John. The fresco had faded slightly from its original glory, but the women's faces were finely drawn and evocative. Lorenzo crossed himself. He walked to the open square window; below were the simple rows of fruit trees edged with a narrow swathe of herbs and beyond Lorenzo saw a crisp outline of San Marco, just across the basin. Sunlight glistened off the windows and flecks of gold indicated decoration. The stern block of the Doge's Palace sat heavily to the side of the Basilica. It was all just as he had remembered it from this vantage point two years earlier.

He turned with a sigh to address Paolo and noticed that the monk had quietly retreated and left him to his thoughts.

The next morning a Mass was celebrated at San Giorgio. Several Cardinals offered the High Service and the monks' Gregorian chant made the occasion solemnly grand. Afterwards, the company gathered for the dedication of the library. Baldassare Loghena himself was present to answer any questions about his design and to explain the architectural details of the building.

Lorenzo stayed in the background, watching from the edges of the crowds who had been invited to have the first view of the masterpiece. He walked through the aisles of shelves that held sacred volumes and which displayed ancient books opened to pages of particularly elegant illumination. Scrolls were carefully stored in an ingenious cubby-hole system and the panelled decorations and details of the fine wood were stunning.

The priest noticed people walking slowly on the perimeters of the rooms gazing at the statues of saints and evangelists nestled in shallow alcoves. He joined the small group just beginning the tour of this feature. The carvings were superb and the polished wood took on the effect of draped fabric, tendrils of beard, and warm flesh. It was phenomenal. Don Lorenzo had heard Paolo mention that the young artist was local to Burano and had surpassed the Northern woodcarvers from Almaine. The woodcarver had become a favorite of Longhena and was busily completing works for him on other projects.

As Lorenzo moved from one figure to the next he noticed particular details on each work that seemed almost a signature of the artist. The position of the hands, the strap of a sandal, or the edge of a cloak seemed distinctive. The statue of Matthew was imbued with a subtle sad reluctance, and Lorenzo was reminded of the humanistic paintings he had seen of Matthew's calling. The beard, the hands, sleeves, even the folds of the neck were so delicately rendered that one could hardly credit the composition as having been created out of wood.

Then he found himself looking at the evocative creation of St. Catherine of Alexandria. The delicate sandaled feet were placed on a carved block of wood fashioned to represent a rough stone. A barely perceptible inscription flowed across carved straps that crossed over a gracefully arched foot. Lorenzo's eyes travelled up the folds of the tunic. The trim was a lacy carving that seemed pierced by the tiniest of needles or woven on bobbins the size of a thimble. The pattern of the lace reminded him of the many linens in the sacristy of his own church in Chioggia, distinctive to his own embroiderer, Faustina Baseggio. The saint clutched the instrument of her martyrdom: the wheel. The details of this wheel created the illusion that it could not have been part of the original block of wood; it was rendered so realistically. Lorenzo was familiar with the several paintings and frescoes of the saint in this pose from churches in Rome. But the gentle features of Catherine's face in this statue seemed to touch him particularly. What was it?

The eyes, though merely the illusion of eyes carved delicately in the wood, looked out at the observer with a calm, intelligent gaze. The expression of sadness and pathos was apparent in the burnished wood despite the gleam and blush in the finish on her sloping cheek. The statues lips were full and slightly curved, not stern. The clear brow was crossed by the bound edge of her veil. Delicately carved curls were visible beneath the veil as it fell on either side of the face. That face… of course. His eyes moved down the draped cloak to the bottom of the statue. He looked closely at the inscription on the sandal strap. He could make out the scripted name of the artist – D. Sarano, but then another symbol, a small rosebud, and the initials E B.

Suddenly Lorenzo realized what he had instinctively known at the first sight of this splendid sculpture. The model for the statue was his own Emilia. The artist must be the young man Emilia had spoken of, her Dario. Of course, D. Sarano. She claimed his work would glorify God and make the world more beautiful.

"Amen," he murmured as he slowly walked down the aisle of the library and out onto the lawns of the island monastery. Lorenzo looked across the basin to the glittering roofs of the grand city of Venice. He could just make out the vertical lines of the columns in the square positioned between the bell tower and the palace. "Amen."

Breinigsville, PA USA
26 October 2009
226486BV00001B/2/P